Blueberry Cobbler Blackmail

Blueberry Cobbler Blackmail

Book 3 in The Cast Iron Skillet Mystery Series

Jodi Rath

Leavensport, Ohio

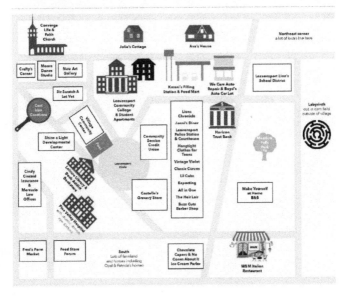

Converge Life & Faith Church

Jolie's Cottage

Ava's House

Northeast corner
a lot of locals live here

Crafty's Corner

Moore Dance Studio

Nuu Art Gallery

Six Scratch A Lot Vet

Leavensport Community College & Student Apartments

Kezzi's Filling Station & Food Mart

We Care Auto Repair & Boyd's Auto Car Lot

Leavensport Lion's School District

Cast Iron Creations

Village Community Center

Shine a Light Developmental Center

Community Service Credit Union

Lions Chronicle

Janni's Diner

Leavensport Police Station & Courthouse

Hangtight Clothes for Teens

Vintage Violet

Classic Curves

Lil Cubs

Expanding All in One

The Hair Lair

Buzz Cuts Barber Shop

Horizon Trust Bank

Labyrinth
out in corn field
outside of village

Cindy Cincaid Insurance & Mercurio Law Offices

Leavensport Public Library & Book Mobile Academy

Pine Valley Hospital

LEAVENSPORT Circle

Castello's Grocery Store

Meadow Public Park

Make Yourself at Home B&B

Fred's Farm Market

Food Store Forum

South
Lots of farmland
and homes including
Opal & Patricia's homes

Chocolate Capers & No Cones About It
Ice Cream Parlor

M&M Italian Restaurant

Familia por encima de todo. Family above all else.

Dedication

Writing a series is a labor of love. It's time-consuming and can take over my entire life. I retreat into my home office and my mind for hours, days, weeks, and months on end. For that reason, I want to thank my husband and our cat family for putting up with that. They love and support me through everything. I'm one blessed woman!

Many of my characters are based loosely on my family. I thank them for allowing that, but also for providing me with limitless humorous anecdotes to use in the books. The relationship that me, my grandma, and my mom have is something else. We are all three strong-willed and strong-headed women who make each other bat-sh** cray cray at times. BUT we would drop everything and do anything for each other. We may be able to talk crap about each other, but anyone else who does— do so at your own peril!

Jolie and Ava—my two favorite gals to write about—Ava is a compilation of all my best girlfriends. All of the bickering between Jolie and Ava—well, that's my BFF Rachel Gruber and me all over! Ava is busty—Leigh Farrington—wink, wink! Ava is sarcastic like my BFF from fifth grade on— Michelle Patrick. Ava and Jolie are a little too close in that they have to talk daily—Rebecca Grubb— texting daily! Jolie can have sweet moments, which always makes me think of my friend, Mary Ann Ware. Delilah's artsy side is inspired by Kim DeKay and Jancy McClellan.

I have to thank my writing groups too! The Eastside Fiction Writers Group meets once a month face-to-face to read and critique. They have opened my eyes to reading other genres, and I've learned so much from all of them about different ways to approach the blank page. Also, Write To Publish, my online writing group does the same for me. It's so great to get to know other writers and get their perspectives on things.

All the women who support me on their blogs, beta readers: Susanna Grubb, Rosie Walton, Michele Wicker, Lauren Dottin, and all the others who have helped in the past—again, I'm a blessed lady!

I have a team of women who put up with all my crazy. I'm a Type-A control freak. Rebecca Grubb is an AMAZING editor and BFF who keeps me grounded. Karen Phillips makes the most amazing covers and deals with all my last-minute changes. And Merry Bond does the formatting on all the books. These women are my rock!

Thanks to all the readers. I wouldn't do this without you. The cozy world is a wonderful place to be!

Exciting News!

***A percentage of all purchases of *Turkey Basted to Death* and *Blueberry Cobbler Blackmail* will be donated to the following two organizations! Thank you for helping those that live with MS and homeless youth! For more information about those navigating life with MS, please visit The MS Society's page at https://www.nationalmssociety.org/ For more information about homeless teens, please visit True Colors United page at https://truecolorsunited.org/

The Leavensport Crew

Jolie Tucker—Co-owner of Cast Iron Creations, born in the village, best friend of Ava, granddaughter of Opal, daughter of Patty.

Ava Martinez—Co-owner of Cast Iron Creations, born in the village, best friend of Jolie, girlfriend of Delilah, sister of Lolly, daughter of Sophia and Thiago.

Keith—Ex-boyfriend of Jolie, born in the village, best friend of Teddy.

Detective Mick Meiser—Love interest of Jolie, from Tri-City, transferred career to Leavensport.

Chief Teddy Tobias—Police chief of Leavensport and born in the village, best friend of Keith.

Lydia—Jolie's frenemy, dating Bradley (or is she?) village nurse, best friend of Betsy, born in the village.

Betsy—Owns Chocolate Capers, best friend of Lydia, born in the village.

Delilah—Sister of Bradley, village artist, girlfriend of Ava.

Bradley—Brother of Delilah, village journalist, dating Lydia--maybe.

Grandma Opal—Jolie's grandma, housewife who helped Jolie and Ava start Cast Iron Creations with her cast-iron skillet recipes.

Aunt Fern—Jolie's wacky, unpredictable aunt, sister to Patty, man-hungry.

Patty—Jolie's mom.

Nestle—Unscrupulous political associate of Mayor Cardinal

Thiago Martinez—Ava's dad

Sophia Martinez—Ava's mom

Theo Sanchez—Lolly's husband

Lolly—Ava's sister.

Carmen and Abraham—housekeeping staff for the Martinez family

Rafi Sanchez—Theo's brother

Ron Rene Sanchez—father of Rafi and Theo, was Thiago's best friend

Franny and Yoselin—run La Franny's Bistro in Santo Domingo

Tink—Jolie's cousin that she only recently realized she had.

Tom Costello—grocer in Leavensport; dating Grandma Opal

Randy—works at record office in Santo Domingo

Chapter One

February 13, 2020

Dear Tabitha,

I'm sorry I was a no-show to our therapy session. Everything was closing in around me. Ava had something develop with her father and needed to hightail it to Santo Domingo ASAP. We scurried to get enough help from our employees and my family to cover the shifts at work. My family is all too willing to do anything for me after the last several months of insanity.

We've been gone close to a month so far, and you would not believe the newest mayhem that has been going on. I am learning that regardless of the outcome, life is a journey of ups and downs and twists and turns. I see how important my course of therapy with you is, and I'm hoping you will be willing to schedule some more sessions when I return.

I've realized—after the numerous life-threatening events that have taken place—I need to figure out what it is I want for my future and work to make that happen. While on—do I dare call it a vacation? I mean, it is paradise here on the island, *but the events have been anything but relaxing. I met this extraordinary guy, and he definitely got my mind off Meiser for a while. It was a breath of fresh air, despite dangerous events, to find someone who I don't have a past with and to have an opportunity to make a new connection without Meiser or Keith around. Well, unless you count Meiser's video calls, texts, and phone calls. . . but otherwise, I've felt a freedom from family and the men in my life like I've never experienced, and it's giving me a new outlook on life!*

I'm looking forward to reflecting on and processing it all when I return to Leavensport.

Sincerely,
Jolie Tucker

The holidays were long over, but I was still feeling the residual stain of grease, mud, and grit eating into my soul. Some people come into our lives and bring nothing but sunshine, while others bring storms. Families, depending on the family, bring shifts in the atmosphere. My current forecast indicates climactic elements that include severe temperature changes, precipitation with gusts of strong winds, hail at times, and the occasional sunny patches. I was feeling that sunny patch right now as I tested out a new cast iron recipe, blueberry cobbler, in the restaurant I co-own with my bestie, Ava Martinez.

I am always most comfortable in the kitchen. There is a wonderful quietude where I can think while being creative with recipes. There is nothing like making fresh dough from scratch and molding it with my hands. The end of January isn't the time of year when blueberries can be found fresh in Ohio, but luckily my grandma had a great relationship with the owners of the local store and farm markets and was able to have some shipped just for me so I can try my hand at a new cobbler with one of my favorite fruits.

My family was walking on eggshells around me, trying to make me happy—namely, my mom, grandma and aunt—after I found out last Thanksgiving that there is this entire other part of our clan that exists that I never knew about. Apparently, long ago, some family dispute took place, and a bunch of them moved to the city, never to be seen, heard from, or spoken of again. At least until late last year when I considered my cousin a suspect for murder. The news hit me like a ton of bricks. I still couldn't believe it two months later. I can only compare it to living my entire life with my soul intact and waking one day to be completely deflated like an exploded balloon with nothing left that shaped me or gave me personality.

Mostly, I'd been living a numb existence, between my family dysfunction and learning Detective Mick Meiser was actually named Mick Milano of the Sicilian Mafia family. But I managed to process that and get over the lies, and when I was finally ready to open my heart to him, he slammed the door in my face by telling me he felt we should be just friends. Both things happened around the same time, making Christmas an extremely joyous occasion to be had. NOT! Did I mention that I cope by being a sarcastic twit?

"Why do you look like that?" Ava asked, barreling into the kitchen with tie-dyed leggings and an oversized neon-yellow shirt.

I froze, head down, hands caked with sticky dough from setting the cobbler up to put in the oven. I shot her a sinister expression. "Like what?" I susurrated.

"Like your mind is a million miles away, and you are on autopilot."

"Oh, because I am," I said simply, turning to wash my hands so I could put the cobbler in the oven.

"Mmm...kay...so why blueberry cobbler in January? You know it was a pain for Mr. Costello to order in fresh blueberries from Michigan." Mr. Costello was our local grocer, who was a recent widower. He reminded me of Walter Matthau in *Grumpy Old Men.* He was short, pleasantly round, with dark hair with grey running through it and a distinguished, rounded face and dark, cheery eyes.

"Grandma Opal didn't mind asking for me."

"You're being a brat. You're too old to act like such a little monster!"

"I believe I've earned that right," I snapped, blue eyes narrowing.

"Maybe momentarily, but it's time to grow up." The bell on the front door jangled, and Ava spun on her hot-pink Nike high-top heels and flounced away.

Only she could get away with saying that to me.

I took a deep breath and looked around my self-decorated kitchen. I'd made a few updates in the last year as money allowed. I hung a rack from the ceiling over the island that held several different-sized cast iron pans. While I still kept the back-wall turquoise, I had a Marrakesh-style pattern bordering the top of each wall that accented the colors not only in the kitchen but in the front of the house as well. This is where Ava's girlfriend, Delilah, had a huge Leavensport community mural as the focus wall to the left when customers walked in. Last year, Ava and I took Delilah's course on mosaic Marrakesh tile work. She is a wonderful teacher in that she doesn't only show her students how to do something, but she also teaches us the culture and history of the practice. I fell in love with studying the Moroccan culture and wanted to employ some of the concepts in my kitchen.

With the cobbler in the oven, I realized it was time to make a list of what we would need in the coming week. I like to shop weekly rather than monthly, like many restaurants do, to keep more fresh foods available. Planning specials and tweaking recipes is one of my favorite things to do, so I get excited when it is time to plan the list. Just in time, too, as Ava's comments had carried in some dark clouds.

"Hey, you should come out here." Her voice sounded strange—like the world was coming to an end. My stomach dropped, and I brushed back the stray frizzy blonde curls from my face as I heard Ava's footsteps coming back toward the kitchen.

I felt my entire body tighten in alarmed anticipation. There were lots of great things about being so close to your best friend that you can guess what the other was thinking. This was not one of those times that I liked knowing what was coming. Ava appeared, looking like someone had died. Her natural warm copper complexion had faded pale with a greenish tint, and her large dark eyes showed a mixture of hate and sorrow.

Walking through the push doors to the front, I jolted to a stop. I couldn't move. Ava ran straight into my back, projecting me forward.

"Sorry," she mumbled.

"NO!" I whirled around and dashed through the kitchen, straight into the tiny office to the side, shoving junk out of the way in a panic to close myself inside.

"Jolie, hey, what are you doing?" My bio dad, Chuck, walked toward me. As in every asspect of my life, he had the gall to barge back into the kitchen, thinking he owned it. Some would think I was melodramatic in my reaction to this man, but he had neglected me not once, but multiple times throughout my life. The psychological abuse felt worse than had he just beaten me physically. Whenever I heard other people talk about a parental figure that left them and they never heard from them again, I always wanted to tell them how fortunate they are. I'm sure I would be exactly like them, thinking that was the worst-case scenario, too, if Chuck had just gone and never come back. I'd learned the hard way that leaving for years on end, then showing up and acting like no time had passed and doing that over and over again for an entire lifetime was WAY worse than just leaving. I wish he would leave for good.

"OUT! NOW!" I kicked a box of old receipts out into the kitchen so I could get the door shut.

Chuck jumped back to avoid the box with stray papers flying out as I slammed the door shut and locked myself in. It seemed I was taking this brat thing to a whole new level.

Curling up on the chair, I wrapped my arms around my knees and rocked back and forth. I hated that he still had this effect on me all these years later.

"You heard her. Get out! She doesn't want to see you or need to see you," Ava yelled.

I pulled my phone out of the top desk drawer, texting my mom that he was here. While I wasn't thrilled with my mom right now, she was my go-to with anything Chuck-related. Even though he had hurt me time and time again, I still had these ping-pong feelings. Patty had zero care for this man. She had no issue with physically removing him if necessary. She'd seen firsthand how he affected me. My mom and grandmother both drove me insane about ninety percent of the time, as I'm completely sure I did the same with them. The thing is, though, when any of us needed each other, we were always there for each other. I may be able to talk trash about my family and friends when they drive me nuts, but anyone else who does it better step way back. Like now.

I buried my spinning head in between my knees, trying to get some order to the things swirling in my head. *I swore I was getting stronger. Ugh, sometimes I feel like such a whiner with daddy issues. I need this to stop. I have to take the time to figure this out with Chuck—it has went on far too long.* I reached out to my mom. I had to figure this stuff out with my family. Ava was right. I couldn't keep shaming them and manipulating them. I was being a child. Also, I needed to figure out what I wanted for my future. I mean, yeah, I co-own a restaurant and I'm only twenty-four, but I can't seem to make a relationship stick with a man. I don't know how to trust men, and the main reason for that was standing on the other side of this door, screaming at my best friend right now.

"YOU STAY OUT OF THIS, AVA! THIS IS NONE OF YOUR BUSINESS! IF I WANT TO TALK

TO MY DAUGHTER THEN THAT HAS NOTHING TO DO WITH YOU!" Chuck yelled, leaning toward Ava.

I felt white-hot rage course through my body. *How dare he yell at her!*

I lugged what felt like five hundred pounds of weight on my shoulders up, turned the knob, and dragged my deflated body out of the office. My mother, all one-hundred-thirty pounds of her, burst through the restaurant door and stopped. My father stood between the two of us as we both tried to glare a hole in him.

Yelling is what I wanted to do. I willed outrage to take over me, but that little girl with her blonde pigtails and mousy voice is what squeaked out, "I told you to leave. Don't yell at Ava. She has done nothing but be there for me. It's so much more than I can say for you. She's more of my family than you ever will be."

Oh boy, here come the waterworks. Same old, same old. Tears welled up in Chuck's blue eyes as his hands began to tremble. I knew what he was getting ready to say and that made the statement that much worse.

"Daddy loves you!"

Ugh.

"OUT, right now, OUT, and I mean it, Chuck," hissed my mother. "I've called Chief Tobias to have him come here and remove you from the property if needs be. I'm not messing around. You have caused enough heartache for five lifetimes. Lord knows why you are back this time. Do you need money again? It's not her job to take care of you, you jack--!" My mom had all the outrage I wished I could muster.

Chuck cut her off in protest, but my mom cut him off as she shoved him hard toward the back door. He's a good fifty pounds heavier than she is, but she is wicked scary when provoked. "Save it, you are sorry, you messed up, you are ready to make amends. Blah, blah, BLECK! No one cares! No one believes you! NO ONE NEEDS YOU HERE!"

She gave one final push, simultaneously opening the door enough for him to stumble out the back. He shrieked, making that sound that sent fear straight through me.

"You are too nice to him. Always have been," my mother, Patty, said, locking the door and moving to gather the receipts that had spilled over. "Make sure you don't lose these," she waved them at me. "You'll need them at tax time!"

"You're the one who married him. I never asked to be born! And I know how taxes work, Mother!" I had no issue mustering up anger toward her. I never had. Although I was aware that she deserved anything but right now.

"Don't give me that load of bull, Jolie. I've told you a million times it was all worth it because I got you. He is not worth anything—you, on the other hand, are worth everything."

Darn it. My shoulders slumped and my eyes began to well up with tears.

"I just got done telling her she's been acting like a spoiled little monster and needs to grow up," Ava said, rubbing my mom's arm.

"Hello, I'm sorry, aren't you supposed to be on my side, you suck-up?" I growled. This is one of the reasons I both loved and hated my closeness with Ava. My family (including Ava) never lets me have a pity party. Which is a good thing, except when I wanted to have a pity party.

"See, what twenty-four-year-old says 'suck-up' anyway? You're proving my point!"

My eyelids tightened and my round cheeks flushed as I moved toward Ava. She saw me coming and squared up, puffing out her chest.

My mom stepped between us and put her hands out to keep us apart. "Girls, do not force me to make a scene in your restaurant!"

We both stopped and stared at each other, huffing. The thing about us is, we are the best of friends and also business partners–that situation can prove to be a little too close for comfort at times. I'm an only child; Ava has a sister, but they were never close growing up. So, Ava and I were more like siblings than friends. We grew up next door to each other, and I'd guess over ninety percent of the time she stayed over at my house or me at hers. We still live next door to each other, too, and ride to work together daily. So, yeah, we grate on each other's nerves often.

BZZZZ!

Saved by the oven timer. The cobbler was done, and I heard my mom's new dog, Colt, barking up front.

"He's not in the restaurant, right?" I carped. "Mirabelle can have Spy in here, since he's her seeing-eye dog. We can't have other pets in here." Mirabelle was Cast Iron Creations' beautiful hostess. She had Down syndrome and dealt with some sight issues, so she had Spy, her seeing-eye dog that sat up front with her as she greeted the guests. She brought a smile to the face of every patron who entered.

"Of course not! I tied him up out front. He's probably spotted a squirrel or something. I mean, do you think I'm an idiot?"

She really shouldn't ask me things like that if she doesn't want to know. I bit my tongue.

"Thanks for coming here," I said crisply. "I need to get a list together of things to purchase for next week's menus, and it will help take my mind off everything."

"Is this your way of telling me to leave?"

I shrugged, putting the cobbler on a cooling rack.

"That's fine. I'll go. Just so you know, young lady, this family will sit down sometime soon to discuss everything that has taken place over the holidays."

Nodding, I turned away as my mother left. More deep breaths. I couldn't take much more. I needed an escape.

"Oh, no! Ava!" I heard my mother shout from out front. What now? I raced out and found Ava slumped on the ground with her cell in her hand. "What happened?" I gasped, sinking down beside her.

"She's crying, and she won't tell me!" My mother had gone into mom mode, running to grab to-go boxes.

"Hi! I am so sorry about this, but we are having an unexpected family emergency." Patty was speaking sweetly but urgently to an elderly couple at a table. "We're going to close the restaurant. Your meal is on me today; we are so sorry to rush you out!"

"Oh, dear," the older gentleman patted Patty's

hand. "Quite alright, but I hope everything is okay."
Patty smiled at him.

"I'm sure it will be just fine." She moved
smoothly to the next table, handing out to-go boxes,
collecting their unpaid bills, smiling, and nodding.

"Hey, that was a switch!" I said, turning to Ava.
"I was the emotional psycho earlier. Were you
trying to reclaim your role as drama queen?" I
asked, trying to make light.

"That was my mom on the phone. You know, the
crazy strong one? Have you ever seen or heard that
woman cry? Well, she's not okay."

My heart sank.

"Is your dad alright? Lolly?" I gulped. Sophia
Martinez was a short, pleasingly curvy woman who
gave my grandma a run for her money when it
came to extreme attitude.

"No one is hurt. I think," Ava stared off into
space, then shook herself back to earth. "No, she
would have told me if someone was hurt."

"Of course, she would have. What's going on?"

"I'm not completely sure. She was crying so hard
it was difficult to make out what she was saying.
She's sending me a link to a video, but she told me I
am NOT to go there. Someone is blackmailing my
father. Something about money troubles or the
business. Someone in the family could be in danger.
She told me if anything ever were to happen to her
and my father that I should take care of Lolly. All I
know is I have NEVER heard my mother cry or
sound like that. She is always in control, and I'm
freaking out. I think I'm having one of those panic
attack things you get." Ava grabbed hold of her
heart, and her eyes bugged out.

"Just take deep breaths with me," my mom said.

She had gotten everyone out, turned the open sign to closed, and locked the door.

Ava's family came from the Dominican Republic to Ohio. Ava and Lolly were born here. Her family had a business there that went back several generations. I never knew why they moved here, but a couple of years ago, Ava's father, Thiago, wanted to move back to Santo Domingo for the business. His daughter Lolly, her husband, and their kids moved with the family, so Theo, Lolly's husband, could be involved with the Martinez business.

Mom helped Ava up to her feet, and we moved to the kitchen. She got her settled in the office and came back out, putting on the kettle for tea. "What's going on?"

"Something to do with her family. It's serious. Sophia was crying, and Ava could barely understand her."

"Uh-oh. Wait, you said she was crying? Are you sure? Do you remember when her mother died? They brought her to live with them toward the end. Her mom was so young. It was so unexpected, so tragic. Sophia was like a soldier. I don't think she shed a tear. She was so strong. If *she's* crying, something is very wrong. You two better plan to get down there ASAP."

"How are we going to make that happen?" I asked as the kettle whistled. "She's not even said she plans to go."

"Between me, your grandmother, your aunt, and your uncles, we can take care of everything here. We can all talk, text, or email as we need help. I'll call everyone. I'm sure Mary will pitch in too."

Mary was Mirabelle's mom. She had filled in to

help us out on multiple occasions.

I couldn't believe my mom said, "uncles," plural. Was she actually acknowledging that I have more than one?

"Mom, take a breath. Let me talk to Ava about all of this first," I said, wondering why she thought I should go, too.

Ava appeared in the office doorway, smiling wanly. "I would really appreciate that, Patricia Rosemary," Ava said, using my mom's full name out of love.

"Of course, dear. You know I think of you as a daughter, too. Lord knows the two of you act like crazy sisters most of the time anyway."

I grinned at Ava. "So, you are planning to go find out what's going on?"

"I have to. I've never heard my mom like that. You stay here and hold down the fort, though," Ava said. I saw her hands shaking.

"I mean, I kind of need to get away with everything that happened the last few months. I'm not used to not having you by my side daily. I guess we could go together, follow my mom's plan if you want. We've become a pretty good team when it comes to figuring out mysteries."

Ava must have been trying to be strong because as soon as I asked, she visibly relaxed and went into go-mode. "I heard the plan. Let's get going." Ava grabbed a cup for tea and set it down on the counter so I could pour it. She started tapping on her phone, her thumbs darting around like frantic mice. "Okay, I'm on the airline website, and there are seats available for the flight we need...hold on." More tapping. "Okay. I booked us two tickets for Santo Domingo. Done. Our flight leaves in the morning."

"Got it," I said, then turned to my mom. "The cats?"

"I've got Colt. I know you won't crate them with Dr. Libby. I'll call her and see what we can figure out. There's a good possibility someone in the family could stay with them."

"Jolie, can you come up front with me?" Ava asked.

"What's up?" I asked as Ava turned her voice down a few decibels to keep my mom from hearing.

"I need to run to the bank before they close. I am not completely sure what mom meant about money. I want to see what equity I have in my house and if I can borrow against it if I need to. I don't know how much to tell them."

I felt like icy water had been poured down my back. This suddenly became real. *We might have to exchange our assets for the life of someone we love. Our houses, the restaurant...how much do we have? How much were we worth? Was it enough?*

"Tink," my mother said, walking up front.

I stared.

"Your cousin." she prodded.

"I know who he is, Mother."

"Oh dear, not this 'Mother' crap again. He could watch the cats while you are gone."

"Listen, I appreciate that you high-tailed it over here today with Chuck. Also, you were wonderful with Ava, as always. And don't think I didn't notice that you stuffed a wad of cash in the register to cover all the meals. Now, you are taking care of things while we are gone..." *Good Lord, I really was a complete spoiled little brat!* "BUT, I'm not sure I'm ready to let this person stay in my house with my family for who knows how long?"

"This *person*, as you refer to him, is your cousin, Jolie Lynn, and he will be a part of your life moving forward. Now, I am sorry all of this happened. Yes, you had a right to be angry, and I understand why you've been taking things out on us. We are not a perfect family. No family is, young lady. I have missed my brother, and I have an opportunity to bring this family back together. It *will* happen. In time."

"I'm not ready to discuss this," I said briskly. "We have a lot to cover before I go home to pack."

"Well, good. Let's get going then."

"My cats!"

"Board them at the vet!"

Crossing my arms, I glared at my mother.

"Don't pout at me, girlie. Tink or board."

I had no time to deal with this. "Will you, Grandma, Aunt Fern, and Uncle Wylie check on them daily? You will tell him all the routines?"

"Yes, and yup! It's settled. Now, let's get this list going. I need to know when people get their paychecks to make sure they get their money."

Geez, I want to be a mom someday so *I* can always win.

🌑

Driving to the Tri-City airport at two a.m. was not my cup of tea. Well, Ava was driving. I was sitting with my head against the window watching Leavensport pass me by and trying not to doze off.

I perked up as we were heading toward the highway, and I saw M&M's Italian Restaurant.

Mick's restaurant had beautiful pale-yellow landscape lights that surrounded the building and the property. It set a romantic mood at nighttime. I know it was the middle of the night, but it reminded me of Mick. I had opted not to go to his house. No time. I could have called, but I didn't.

We whizzed past the restaurant to where the miles and miles of fields and woods lay before us, leading us toward the city. A huge sign was back up that lots were for sale. I jerked my head around to make sure what I saw next was real and not a figment of my imagination. I swear it looked like a shadow was digging in the field near Meiser's restaurant.

Chapter Two

February 1, 2020

"Did your mom send you the link to the video?" I asked as we were settling in for our seven-hour flight to Santo Domingo. Ava did not tell her family we were on our way there since she knew her mom would not be happy. I had never been there before, but Ava had visited with her family as a child and again when she was a teen. She brought a ton of pictures to show me, and despite the grim reasons we were headed there, I was relieved for the break from my family and the chance to explore a new place.

Between me working with my family to go over as much as I could to cover the restaurant and her gathering a way to get money, Ava had barely any time to talk. Tink had showed up that night to get the first-hand scoop from me on the kitty routine.

At first, I was trepidatious about him being there, but once I saw how much all four cats took to him, including Sammy Jr, who hid from everyone but me, I felt a lot better. Although it did grate at me to watch my mother get such satisfaction from it. Ava had secured some money she could borrow against and have wired. Denise, who was Keith's sister and a credit union teller, had done a ton in a short amount of time. She covered most of the preparation at our appointment at the bank the afternoon before, just a few hours after we had found out we needed to leave. She said anything else that came up we could deal with from Leavensport while we were in Santo Domingo. Ava called me around midnight to tell me she was picking me up at 1:30 a.m.

"You realize that is in a little over an hour, right?" I muttered.

"Yes!" she practically yelled. "Get packing!" She had enough anxious energy for both of us.

Then before we knew it, we were on the plane.

"Yeah, I've watched it several times. It's some douche in a mask with a distorted voice, and they have wavy lines going through the video to hide their identity. I mean, cowards!" Ava said a little too loudly. The plane wasn't packed, but a few heads rolled around as sleepy eyes looked our way.

"Wait," I asked, confused. "Why did she send you the video? She told you to stay in Leavensport."

"She actually kind of recognizes that we have had some success in solving crimes in the past. She sent it to me, asking if we can figure anything out in the video. From Ohio, of course."

"She's going to be ticked when we show up there," I said. "I want to see it. I brought my laptop so we can do our I Spy Slides. Let's add the video into the slide and take some notes."

"Don't you want to sleep on the way?" asked Ava.

"Oh, yeah, sure, we can if you want to."

"No, I'm not saying I don't want you to see it. You're doing a lot for me. If you need to sleep, then sleep. You can watch this later."

"Oh boy, plleeeazzze do not get all nicey-nice with me," I groaned. "I've dealt with all this family drama, Chuck, Keith, and Meiser, and that is not even getting into all the crime and how many times I've come close to death in the last year. So, the last thing I need is for you to be acting like a sentimental dope."

Ava looked like I slapped her in her face, then her cheeks puffed out, and she turned away, looking out the window. "Once a spoiled brat, always a spoiled brat!"

"Just show me this creep's video," I said, firing up my Surface and opening the PowerPoint we used.

Ava cued up the video on her phone.

"No, send it to me so I can put it on the computer, and we can see it on a larger screen to see if we can recognize anything."

"Just watch it here first," she said, hitting play. We each had one earbud in so we wouldn't disturb other passengers.

Like Ava said, it looked like this person was all in black with a mask and a distorted voice. The picture was blurry and had squiggly lines going through it, making it impossible to focus on anything.

Roses are Red, Violets are Blue.

The great Thiago Martinez is not so big anymore.

Your husband has again been up to no good.

Check your accounts. Ask him why this is.

Your family should have stayed in the States.

Your family will get $50,000 to me by the Valentine's Day holiday.

El destierro tiene un costo.

XOXO

"He's not very good at poetry, is he?" I asked.

"Why do you say 'he?'"

"I guess I don't know for sure, but I have a feeling it's a man."

"Don't do that."

"Why?"

"Hey, I'm sending this to you...put it in our I Spy Slides," Ava said. My phone buzzed. "It's best if we don't identify with a specific gender if we don't know for sure," she continued. "I learned that in my online PI course. If you continually say 'he,' then you subconsciously only suspect men, when it could just as easily be a woman."

I pursed my lips in contemplation, "Makes sense. You're really enjoying those courses, huh?"

"Yeah, I'm feeling more empowered. Somehow, we've got ourselves intertwined in so many situations the last year. It feels good to take some action. Plus, with all this mess, I'm hoping some of the things I've learned will help my *familia.*"

"What was the Spanish line he, er, they said?"

"Banishment has a cost."

I uploaded the video to the PowerPoint and made a note of that below. I also noted that I had a feeling it was a man and glanced over at Ava, who was rolling her eyes at me. "So, the things this person says, it feels personal."

"Yeah, they sent it to my mom. They call my dad

'great,' but they obviously mean anything but."

"They knew your family was in Santo Domingo, moved to the States, and came back. Plus, they know something about accounts—plural. The question is, does plural mean their personal checking and savings only, or the business accounts, too?"

"Make a note about the poetic line and Valentine's Day. That is weird. That gives us two weeks to get the money. That seems like a big cushion, doesn't it?"

"I don't know. I've never been blackmailed before." I was biting my nails back from nerves. "I'm adding the line about banishment. We need to ask your family about that."

I took a moment to think back to last Valentine's Day. Meiser and I had tried to go away for a romantic weekend—which turned out to be anything but. This year I would be alone in a different country attempting to solve yet another crime.

"Yeah, that line is the key to this whole video," Ava said.

"Wait, I thought you weren't supposed to make assumptions?"

"Nah, this one is okay."

"What did Delilah say?"

"She was amazing, as always. I told her everything too. She wanted to come with us, but I told her we got this. She even told me to call her if we need help with more money."

"Yep, she is too good for you. I've always said it."

"You're an idiot."

"When are you going to put a ring on it?"

"I'm actually thinking about that."

"Whoa, I was only kidding!"

"I'm not. It's been on my mind for a bit. After seeing her go into action for me today, it makes me want to take the leap and settle down."

"Well, we are at that age where people begin to get married and think about a family," I said, realizing how far from that I was. Not that I wasn't thinking it or wanting it, just that I had no real opportunities. Ava seemed to be thinking about this, too, and the silence stretched long. I felt myself getting sleepy. My mind wandered to Meiser, the restaurant . . .

We dozed off the rest of the way.

Ava's sister Lolly met us at the airport, and I saw Ava breathe a big sigh of relief. I assumed it was because her mother or father wasn't there to pick us up. Not ready to deal with them yet. I got it. Ava had told Lolly we were coming, but she gave her sister a direct order to NOT tell their parents. We both weren't sure if Lolly would abide by the order or not. Obviously, she did.

"I can't believe you booked a hotel room. Really? The family is having financial issues, and you book a hotel like you are on some luxury vacation?" Lolly snapped. She grabbed the lightest duffle bag and raced to her car, illegally parked out front.

An officer was walking around her car. He had a notebook with him and was getting ready to open it.

"Oh, sorry, sir. I'm Lolly Martinez-Sanchez. My sister is in from the States visiting. She phoned that there was an emergency, and she needed me at the airport ASAP. I'm so sorry for parking here," she grabbed something out of her purse and put both her hands over his, looking him straight in the eye.

The officer said nothing, turned, and pocketed some gold coins. I assumed they were pesos, but who knew, since the Martinez business was gold.

"Emergency? You just bribed an officer!" Ava threw my suitcase into the trunk.

"Hey, I have some breakables in there, be careful!" I protested.

"Also, I booked a hotel room because I am a grown adult, Lolly," Ava snapped back. "I don't need to rely on Mama and Papa to take care of me. I don't need to live where they live to get my *significant other* a job."

So much for Ava's sigh of relief.

"I don't need anyone to do anything for me. I'm so perfect in every way," Lolly mimicked.

"That's rich. I mean, seriously rich! You're calling *me* perfect! Little Miss Can't Do Anything Wrong Ever. Hetero Lolly, with her supposedly perfect husband and giving *Mami* and *Papi* grandchildren. All A's, prom queen, 4.0 college graduate in business. Daddy's little princess," Ava practically spit.

The officer began walking back toward us. The three of us jumped in the car, and Lolly roared off.

As Lolly and Ava quietly fumed on the trip to our hotel, I was wide-eyed in amazement as we drove along the coast looking over the Caribbean Sea. I was pretty sure it was the sea. I am geographically challenged. Atlantic Ocean, maybe? Hmmm . . . I'd like to ask, but the air could be cut with a knife right now, so I decided best to drool over the white sand beaches and palm trees! Oh wow, I'd only ever seen pictures before. I sat up straight and started glancing back and forth, looking from Ava to Lolly. Ava gave me an odd look.

We got to our hotel. It was a beautiful hotel featuring historical architecture. I was surprised that Ava said it was one of the less expensive in the area. The others on the strip seemed to be more modern and taller. This one was built like a ranch-style house, except much larger. The walls were stone with heavy wooden doors. There was a central garden that had a pond with an archway over it that was dark mahogany wood. It had large colorful blown glass floats of ducks on the water. There was a huge, blue-tiled pool for the patrons. We got settled in as Lolly stood in the corner, tapping her foot impatiently. The moment we had put our luggage away, Lolly dragged us back to the car to head for the Martinez home. I looked longingly at the bed before we headed out.

I immediately perked up as Lolly hit a button that opened an iron fence, and we entered a long lane winding up to one of the most gorgeous properties I'd ever laid eyes on. Lolly parked alongside a luxuriously rustic three-story terracotta villa. There was lush green grass and a cobblestone walk leading to a beautiful flower garden with vibrant colors of plants, bushes, and trees I'd never seen before. There was a small pond with trees surrounding it and a perfectly placed wooden bench.

"Ava!" The woman who opened the door was shocked to see us. "You are here! I did not know that you were coming. Your mother will be...so surprised."

"Hello, Carmen," Ava said. "Sorry to startle you." The forty-something year old woman was dressed in a floral printed top and matching pants with sandals. She beckoned them in.

"Miss Ava, so good to see you again," Carmen wrapped Ava in her arms. "I will go tell your *mami* and *papi* that you and your friend are here."

I smiled at Carmen and followed Ava. Lolly went up the steps near the door without saying a word. Come to think of it, I'm not sure that Lolly had said one word to me. You're *welcome* for being there for your sister, I thought to myself!

"Who was that?"

"Carmen, my family's cook."

"Your family lives here and has their own cook?" I asked incredulously.

"They have a butler, cook, maid, and gardener too."

"Whoa, hold up. Stop moving. Must take this in," I felt like I had brain-freeze.

"Calm down."

"Huh, your family lived in a tiny cottage in Leavensport and drove sensible cars. Now, we are in a castle in paradise with servants?"

"Please don't call them servants, Jolie," shushing me and grabbing my arm, Ava moved me into a gigantic library with shelves going from floor to ceiling on three walls.

She sat me on an unbelievably comfortable, beautifully upholstered, sea-blue chair. I could have curled up and read one of the thousands of books. I could live in this chair!

"Sorry," I said awkwardly. "I didn't know that was the wrong thing to say."

"In the Dominican Republic, there are still enslaved people. Trafficking is bad too. My family has a history of working to advocate to free the people who are enslaved. They aren't very popular for it. Carmen and Abraham are two people who *were* enslaved, and Papa worked tirelessly to get them freed. They live here with the family now and work for us."

"Wow," I said, in awe. "It's like you have a whole other life I know nothing about. I really am shallow."

"No, I don't live this life. I only know about it because they are my family. Obviously, there is a lot I *don't* know, given the reason we are here. Now, get your lazy butt up and let's head out back."

We had to walk through the kitchen to get to the deck out back. I'm not sure "deck" is the appropriate word. "Heaven on earth" described it better. We walked through sliding doors to a pastoral wooden veranda with bamboo roofing and arched open windows framing a gorgeous vista of the water. Sea? Or ocean? Man, I needed to brush up on my geography. A hammock hung to the left with shelves of clay-potted plants by one huge window. Long pink draperies reached to the floor on the right with graceful vines climbing around them. The furniture looked handmade: chunky dark wood with lavishly thick cushions in floral pink, green, and terracotta swirls. The windows on the other side overlooked a small yard with a pink-tinted shed on the far edge. One beautiful plant taller than my own five-foot-seven frame stood in the middle of the yard, and surrounding the greenery were perfectly manicured bushes.

"AVA!" Sophia erupted through the door. "What are you doing here?"

"Hello, *Mami*," Ava said calmly. "It is good to see

you. Aren't you going to say hello to Jolie?"

"Hello, Jolie, my dear," Sophia hugged me rather roughly, then turned back to her daughter. "Ava, I have told you what is going on here. It may not be safe. Why would you come here?"

"I couldn't just sit there in Ohio, doing nothing," protested Ava, sounding a bit like a small child in trouble.

Sophia took a deep breath and straightened her shoulders. She smiled. "Well, you are here now. So let's get you settled."

"Your home is so beautiful," I spoke up, trying to smooth out the tension. "I'm beside myself."

"Well, thank you, darling!" Sophia beamed. "Have a piece of fresh fruit. Rafi picked it and brought it today. Enjoy it before I scold you and Ava for disregarding my wishes."

"Thank you," I selected what looked to be a bunch of grapes. Turning to Ava, I asked, "Does Rafi work for your family too?"

"No, I do not cater to the Martinez family," said a voice from behind me. "I am Theo's lowly brother. I don't qualify to work for Thiago or his beautiful wife." I turned to find a handsome man with thick, coal-black hair and piercing, bright-blue eyes bowing to me.

"I apologize, I'm—"

"No need for apologies, it is a common mistake to think everyone works for the Martinez family here in beautiful Santo Domingo."

"Knock it off, Rafi," Theo walked out with Lolly on his arm.

It looked like the marriage counseling was working for them.

Rafi stepped back and changed the subject. "While you are here, you should be sure to visit the Three-Eyes National Park. It's beautiful this time of the year. It is the place where I broke my first bone. Theo and I argued, and he pushed me off a cliff, breaking my arm."

This was awkward.

"It wasn't a cliff. You make it sound like I pushed you over. We argued, wrestled, and you tumbled down a little way." Theo rolled his eyes. More sibling rivalry. And I had always wanted a brother or sister. Not now!

Three young versions of Theo and Lolly came running through the doors with water guns, squirting at each other. I got caught in the crossfire and soaked to the bone.

"You three know you cannot do that here. Go out in the yard right now!" Sophia scolded the children, pointing with a perfectly manicured nail, polished a vivid coral color.

"Oh dear," Carmen said, rushing out with a large, soft towel. "The little ones get cabin fever, I'm afraid. You are drenched, dear."

"It's okay. It's warm, and I'll dry. Thank you for the towel."

"I see you chose some limoncillo. You will enjoy," Carmen said.

"I thought they were grapes." I blushed.

"Similar, a bit more tart. Do you like sour taste?"

I popped one in my mouth and felt the juices explode onto my tongue. It was sweet, sour, and reminded me of a sweet dessert wine crossed with a sour patch kid. Yum! My eyes must have lit up because Carmen smiled at me, satisfied as I nodded.

"Where is Papa?" Ava asked.

"He is finishing up some business in his office. He will be down soon," Sophia said.

"Jolie, come with me and let's find you something to change into," Ava said, pulling me into the house and leading me up the marble-tiled steps. "I swear, I can't take you anywhere."

"What? Your little niece and nephews did this to me. I'm the victim here."

"Everyone knows to duck and cover when those little turds show up."

"It would have been nice if someone would have warned *me*!"

"Well, now you know." Ava led me into a spare bedroom, where she began looking through a large dresser stuffed with clothing. "Here's a T-shirt and a pair of shorts to throw on. Carmen can put your things in the dryer so you can change back before we leave. I'm bigger than you, here's a—"

Ava stopped abruptly when we heard Thiago yelling down the hallway. We both hurried toward the door and peeked out to see if we could see him. No one in the hallway. Ava led me, sloshing, down the narrow passage toward her father's deep voice. It sounded as though he was getting more agitated by the second.

"How am I supposed to come up with that? There's nothing left. The authorities don't seem at all concerned with helping our family. What do you expect me to do? He's saying he will do something to my family. How soon could I sell the place?"

Ava looked at me with concern, then pushed me back toward the room. My shoes were squeaking from the water. "Would you be quiet!" Ava hissed.

"I can't help it. Don't push so hard!"

"What are you two doing out here?" Thiago stood hands on hips. He looked like a shorter version of Antonio Banderas with tight, short, curly, black hair. Every time I'd ever seen that man, he had dress slacks, shiny leather shoes, belt, and a crisp button-down shirt. He was well put together for sure.

"Papa, Jolie brought a limoncillo to a water gun fight, and I was just bringing her up to find some dry clothes."

"Ah, the three terror triplets soaked you, I see," Thiago moved toward his daughter and hugged her tightly. He turned to me, considering a hug but settling for a nod.

"Ava, why did you not listen to your mother. We were not expecting you here. When Carmen told me you had shown up at our door..." Thiago glared at both of us, but in a warm-hearted fatherly way.

I did an awkward wave and moved to the room to change so Ava could catch up with her dad.

I left my tote downstairs. It had my laptop in it. I wanted to make notes about some of the things Rafi said earlier. Also, the things we just overheard with Thiago should be noted, too. Ava was about two sizes larger than me in all the right places, so I had to cinch the belt around my waist, but the tee was oversized and comfy.

I headed downstairs and through the kitchen.

"Tea, Miss Jolie?" Carmen asked.

"Yes, please."

"Here you go, Miss."

"Oh, it's iced tea?"

"Yes, Miss. Bubble tea."

"Bubble tea?"

"You like tea?"

"I love tea—both hot and iced."

"Bubble tea is a blend of black tea, sweetened milk, and boba—black tapioca pearls. You can find it everywhere now. It originated in Taiwan, but the tapioca pearls are made from the cassava root, which is grown here in the Dominican Republic. It is very tasty, no?"

I planned to take a tiny sip to try but ended up sucking down half the glass. Carmen had put a wide straw in the glass so that every so often, I sucked a scrumptious chewy pearl into my mouth. "Wow. This is delicious! It's fruity!"

"Yes, we add fresh fruits to it." Carmen's smile expanded into her cheekbones, showing age lines. She had a strong face with a complexion like a harvest moon. She was beautiful. I couldn't imagine the horrors she must have faced in the past. They didn't show on her kind face.

"You have a gift for preparing food. By the way, I love this room more than any other in the house," I said, sinking onto one of the tall, handcrafted wooden chairs with comfy dark-green cushions on each. The side of the island was a natural grayish stone extending to a marble top. Above it, hung low, was a large, modern, stainless-steel lighting fixture. The extra-large pieces of tile were an acorn brown that matched the stools. Sections of the walls were also beautifully tiled in marble. A full wall was dedicated to the stainless-steel appliances separated by stone dividers that jutted up from the counter at intervals that matched the wall of the island, a large sink, and they had shelving above with custom mahogany cabinetry. It was so natural-looking and beautiful.

"Yes, Miss Sophia tells me about you and Miss Ava and your cast iron restaurant. You know, we use cast iron for cooking here, too."

"You do? Maybe there will be time for you to show me some of the local recipes? I'd love to cook in here with you if you'd allow me to."

"Of course, my child. You are more than welcome to cook for the family," Carmen chuckled.

Sarcasm. Carmen is my kind of woman. I laughed with her.

She filled up my bubble tea, and I walked out to where Ava's family were sucking down their own teas.

"Why didn't you bring me one?" Ava demanded.

Shoulder-shrug, and I kept slurping on my new favorite drink.

"So, why do you think it is the Peréz family, Papa?" Ava asked.

I had obviously walked into the middle of a conversation.

"There's a history between our families, *mija.* I'm not going into it all now. Five generations of our family have been in the gold business and mining. It is where our money comes from. It is hard work, and at times has proven to be dangerous work. In the past, the Peréz family wanted to monopolize on it. Things happened as they always do in feuds. That's a big reason why your mother and I were uprooted and landed in Ohio. Things calmed down. It's the tides of life. We are back—not long before the tides shifted again."

I noticed Rafi roll his eyes as he reached for more fruit, then he seemed fixated on staring at Lolly and Theo, who were holding hands on a love seat across from him.

"Manswer," I mumbled, mimicking Ava's phrase.

"Excuse me, young lady, you are in my home now," Thiago scolded me.

"Don't get stern with her, Papa. She has sacrificed a lot to be here with me. She didn't blink an eye when I went to secure money on the equity in our restaurant."

"What do you mean 'a loan against the restaurant'?" Thiago turned toward his wife. "Did you tell her to do this?"

"I knew nothing about it, *mi corazón.*"

"Papa, Mama called me and gave me an overview of what was going on. That's all. She did not ask me to do anything. She demanded I not come. She wanted me to know she loved me and that I should take care of Lolly if anything happened to you and her. She didn't give me many details. I don't have money with me, but I can get it wired if need be."

"You won't need to. I am the man of the family. I will take care of all this. You and Jolie did not need to leave your work. It seems you are head of your household since you are single."

"You know I'm with Delilah," Ava said, gritting her teeth.

That was another sore spot. Ava's family was as kind as could be to Delilah, but they made Ava aware of the fact that they did not approve. Yet another reason Ava and Lolly did not get along well.

"Lolly, can we talk?" I overheard Rafi whisper

behind me. Theo had gotten up to move to a table to give Carmen a good spot to put the pitcher of bubble tea, and Rafi must have taken that as his opportunity to approach her.

I shifted my weight to get a better view.

"Not here, and not now. Don't touch me!" she seethed, pulling her arm away and walking toward Theo, who, based on the expression I saw on his face, also saw the exchange between his brother and wife.

"Ava, there is nothing you can do now," Sophia sighed. "We have communicated with the blackmailers and made it clear that we will meet their demands. Now we are just waiting for instructions. There is nothing more we can do at this time. You and Jolie work so hard and do not vacation. Why don't you take your friend to the gorgeous beaches to relax a bit?" Sophia tried to change the topic and get rid of us to keep another family feud from brewing.

Ava looked over at me speculatively.

"Sounds good to me." I slurped down the last of my bubble tea.

●

"So how are Lolly and Theo doing now? Things seemed better." Ava's sister and her husband were having marriage issues during the holiday season. Theo had cheated on Lolly, but last I had heard they decided to go to couples therapy to work on the marriage.

"To hear Mama and Papa tell it, she is as perfect as ever. Perfect wife, daughter, data entry assistant for the business, mother—sounds like the marriage is perfect too—like there was never a blot to begin with."

Lolly and Ava have had a sibling rivalry since childhood. Thiago and Sophia Martinez were strict, routine-oriented, and organized. Lolly followed suit with their parent's rules. It is why she had her family pick up their lives in Tri-City to move to Santo Domingo when the Martinezes made the move. Thiago and Sophia expected Ava to do the same. There was a reason Lolly was the favorite, and Ava wasn't.

"It doesn't matter if they all want to pretend there were no problems—we all know better. Plus, I grew up with you and Lolly, I know she is not perfect by a long shot." I reached for the beach bag to add more sunscreen to my shoulders and face.

"Yeah, she's far from perfect in my book. Why are you putting more sunscreen on? You already have the largest-brimmed hat I've ever seen in my life with long sleeves, pants, and huge sunglasses. Not to mention, you are on bottle number two, and we've only been out here one hour." Ava grabbed the bag and pulled it away from me.

"Okay, first of all, you're being overdramatic again. Second, I burn. I don't have a beautiful chestnut skin tone that only gets deeper and more beautiful when I lay in the sun. One hour in the sun for me equals me looking like a lobster that was dyed blood red, because, for some reason, his natural red wasn't good enough." I jerked at the beach bag to get it out of Ava's hand, and the contents of my bag flew out. My journal landed on the blanket with the letter to Tabitha hanging out of it. The letter blew free in the breeze, slowly tumbling and drifting across the white sand. I grabbed at it and missed. I scooted forward on my knees and grabbed at it again, missing by inches.

Before I knew it, I was chasing it on hands and knees, like a baby crawling for the first time, simultaneously trying to hold my humongous hat on with one hand.

"Ow." I had hit my head on something. The letter had stopped moving! Because whatever I had crashed into was pinning it down...a foot? A tanned hand reached down to pick up the letter.

"Are you okay?"

I followed the foot up to see an absolutely gorgeous man with thick, long wavy black hair. He was shirtless, and his stomach was way beyond a six-pack—try a ten-pack. His pecs were just incredible. I had never seen anything like it. And his biceps—tanned, glistening, and he wasn't even flexing! I was on hands and knees staring at his body, and I realized I was drooling, although my mouth felt parched as the desert. How is that possible? My brain moved in slow motion. *This guy is what Greek gods are modeled after.*

"I-I-I," I stammered like I didn't know English.

"Jolie, stand up," Ava hissed, grabbing my elbow. "You are making a fool of yourself." Luckily, for once, she didn't yell what she said for all to hear. She helped me to my feet.

"I am so sorry. I must seem crazy," I reached up to run my fingers through my shoulder-length curly, blonde hair, forgetting I had a wide-brimmed hat on. I knocked it off, and the wind caught it. I turned to run after it, but Ava grabbed my elbow to stop me. Handsome beach guy had rushed away suddenly.

"Look, Adonis there is going after your hat! Wow. This is like an episode of Dominican Baywatch. Slow down, baby, slow down for Mama."

Ava stared and fanned herself.

"You're gay!" I exclaimed.

"I can make an exception!" Ava's mouth was hanging open as Adonis came jogging back with my ridiculous, floppy sun hat.

I elbowed her hard in her side, and she grunted and bent double, then while she was down there, she pinched the flab on the back my thigh. "Ouch!" I slapped her.

"What could be wrong with two of the most beautiful women in all the Dominican Republic?" Adonis asked, with white teeth glistening.

"She's a klutz. Drops everything, can't stand straight," Ava said, miming a drunken stagger that was intended to reference me.

I rolled my eyes, and Adonis handed me my hat. He made a point to brush my hand as he did so.

"You both tourists on vacation here?"

"My family lives here. I've visited before, though. We're from the States," Ava said, sidling up to him.

Ava was a bountiful woman. She had big curves in all the right places. She had a tiny bikini on as she had no issues being a beautiful plus-sized queen.

I grabbed her by the shoulder and moved her back, "She's got a girlfriend back home."

Ava glared at me. Too bad.

"Ah, and you?" Adonis asked.

"I'm single *and* straight."

"This is nice to know. Well, fortunately for you both, you have run into the number one tour guide of Santo Domingo. Now, I know your family lives here," Adonis looked to Ava, "but I have much knowledge of the history of this beautiful place. You and your friend should take a tour with me tomorrow. I will give you both a private tour, so you get better attention."

His phone buzzed, and he glanced at the screen, his expression changing instantly from charming to terrified. He rushed to grab it and moved away from us quickly.

Ava and I raised our eyebrows at one another. It was an odd reaction after he was so suave before.

Adonis had his back to us and hung up quickly. I noticed that he took a huge breath before he turned around. He gave us a sparkling smile and resumed being Mr. Wonderful.

"So sorry, ladies. So we do a tour tomorrow, yes?"

"Oh, I don't think we—" I began.

"Of course," Ava interrupted. "Where should we meet you and what time? I would love to take lots of pictures."

"But of course. Pictures are a must! Meet me at La Franny's Bistro at ten a.m. Make sure your clocks are set. Where you live in states?"

"Ohio."

"We are one hour ahead. See, I have much knowledge."

"You sure do!" Ava sighed, fanning her face with her hand as Adonis walked away.

"Just what do you think you are doing? How do you know we don't need to do something for your family? That's why we're here!"

"You heard my mother. She couldn't get me out the door fast enough today. We are just waiting right now. What better way to wait than walking around Santo Domingo behind that *papi chulo* and taking pictures of his a—"

"Again, you are in a relationship, *planning to propose!*"

"Oh, I know that! I'm having a little fun. It's harmless." Ava walked in front of me, pulling a wedgie from her tight bikini drawers.

"We don't even know his first name. We can't call him Adonis."

"We'll find out tomorrow. No biggie."

My cell rang. It was a video call from Meiser.

I picked up as I was putting my hat back on.

"Well, hello, Audrey Hepburn. I see a little vacation brings out your celebrity side." Meiser looked amused.

Ava cackled out loud. I glared.

"I'm pale," I stated the obvious.

"Why didn't you tell me you were leaving?" He brushed his hand through his thick and wavy brown hair that had some silver strands running through it and stared at me with those large brown eyes framed with long eyelashes. This caused me to forget all about Adonis.

Once I stopped drooling and realized he asked me a question, I stared at him, dumbfounded. What was I supposed to say? That I thought about coming to his house, then no, I thought about calling him, then no, I figured he wants little to do with me, so why should I contact him? That would be awkward.

"Jolie, did you hear what he asked you?"

Not helping!

"I, uh, well, I, I just—"

"It's my fault. She's helping my family with a problem. She really didn't need to come, but she's such a great friend."

"What problem?" Meiser asked.

"Just family stuff. You know how that is."

"Oh yeah, I know!" Meiser exclaimed. As much dysfunction as my family faced over the holidays, his was even worse. I'd known little about his family, other than one of his brothers used to be the Mayor of Tri-City. I hadn't even realized that until recently. Part of our issues had to do with his secrets about his family. It turns out Meiser is Milano, and he comes from an Italian Mafia family. "How are things going with your family?"

"Could be better or worse," I said.

"Your grandma keeps texting me."

My eyes bugged out of my head. "What? Why?"

"She has discovered GIFs. She favors the ones featuring Benny Hill."

"Again, why?"

"Don't you know? Italians love Benny Hill."

Ava and I stared at each other. She shrugged her shoulders.

"Again, why?" I asked.

"We love slapstick comedy more so than acerbic sarcasm."

"You must love scantily clothed women too," Ava said.

"I could definitely be into that, given the right woman." Meiser burrowed a stare into my soul.

"We gotta go." I turned the call off.

"Yowsa, someone wants to see you naked," Ava said.

"That's not true," I said.

"Didn't you just hear what the man said?"

"He wants to see me *scantily dressed*."

"Well, today would not be a good day."

Chapter Three

The next day we got an Uber and went to La Franny's Bistro to meet Adonis for our tour. We both made sure our phones were charged, and I had the large, brown leather tote that I took with me everywhere. I always had to have books, a journal, and my portable Surface laptop with me. Tabitha, my therapist, thought I could be a tad obsessive-compulsive. Okay, well, she didn't *say* that. I may have mentioned that I have OCD tendencies, and she didn't correct me. Honestly, I'm sure it is something she and I will address in future sessions.

Our Uber driver let us out and pointed us down an alley toward the bistro. The alleyway reminded me of a Caribbean-inspired art walk that we had in Leavensport. Across the alley from our restaurant was where the museums, dance studio, and craft store were located. It had a beautiful brick and cobblestone walk so patrons could walk along and window-shop and feel cozy and at home. We walked up the stone slab walkway under the thatched roof. Along the walls, there were royal blue, red, and white flowers in a design resembling the flag of the Dominican Republic. La Franny's Bistro sat behind this floral wall.

Adonis stood at the counter, drinking a bubble tea. I wasn't sure which to drool over. The two ladies working at the counter seemed to choose Adonis. Good taste.

"Hello, ladies," Adonis grinned. "Come, come, let me introduce you to the two beautiful, best cooks in all Santo Domingo." I was sensing a theme with Adonis. "This is Franny and Yoselin. They co-own this bistro. And this is the lovely Ava and her gorgeous friend, Jolie. Ava's family lives here."

Ava and I stared at each other and smiled, happy to see two other boss babes co-own a restaurant. Their place was cute. It was much smaller than ours. There were only four tables up front, a counter with fountain drinks behind it, then, I presumed, the kitchen was in the back. It was completely closed off from the front, unlike our setup, which allowed me to see the front through the kitchen window and the push door.

"And what is your name?" I asked Adonis.

"Ah, yes, I never did get to that, did I? I am Kayden Rodríguez. The pleasure is all mine, ladies," Adonis held out his manly hand.

Ava grabbed his hand, holding on for dear life.

"We co-own a restaurant in the States," I said, turning to Franny and Yoselin.

They glanced at each other and smiled too. Some looks translate across countries.

"What's the name of your restaurant?" Yoselin asked.

"Cast Iron Creations," Ava said.

"See, a neutral name. Not one name over the

other," Yoselin rolled her eyes at Franny.

I see relationships with these two similar to what Ava and I have going on.

"I like 'La Franny Bistro.' It has a nice ring to it," Ava said, eyeing me.

I shook my head.

"I run the front house. I'm the face people see. Yoselin cooks," Franny said.

"Same," Ava said.

"Would we know your family?" Franny asked Ava.

"The Mart--," Ava started to say.

I noticed Franny looked momentarily panicked, then Yoselin interrupted.

"I do more than just cook," Yoselin protested.

"Me too!" I gave Yoselin a knowing look, which she graciously returned.

"Well, I will say if you are looking for a fabulous meal, you should come here. These ladies will take good care of you," Adonis—er—Kayden said.

"I'd love to take a look at the back at some point," I said to Yoselin.

"Of course. I even have some cast irons back there. I'm happy to show you some demonstrations of some of our specials if you find you have the time. Also, you seem to be the quiet one, like me. You should visit the Fortaleza Ozama to reflect on the things of life. The Dominicans eventually wised up and learned to protect themselves. Kayden here can fill you in on our rich history."

"I hope to. We are not on vacation," I said.

"Why are you here, then?" Franny asked.

I looked at Ava.

"As Kayden said earlier, my family is here," she explained. "We are helping them with a few things. But we will have some time here and there. Like today."

"Yes, we best be going," Kayden said.

"Be careful, that stray is outside looking in again," Franny said distastefully.

"Oh my gosh, he's adorable," I said, walking toward the door. A large orangish-yellow-and-white cat was pawing at their window. I turned. "He doesn't look like a stray."

"People up and down the alley feed him," Yoselin said, running back to the kitchen.

Walking out the door, I bent down to pet him. He looked up at me with his huge eyes, and I petted him as he purred loudly. Yoselin came out behind me with some soft food in a bowl.

"Franny is not an animal person. I feed him daily around this time. Do you have pets?"

"I have four cats. I'm an only child, but my mom recently gave me a younger brother named Colt. He's a Chihuahua mix."

Yoselin grinned. She and Franny were both similar in age to Ava and me. Yoselin had long, straight, thick black hair with a citrine complexion. She wore a little make-up, but with big brown eyes, rosy cheeks, and naturally high cheekbones, and a pouty mouth, she looked like a model. For a cook, she looked cool in a southwestern-patterned smock over a midriff turquoise tee and tight-fitting jeans. She was tall and lean, as well. Franny was shorter by a few inches with long, spikey, brown hair that had pink tips. She wore a black, button-up shirt, stretchy, black mini skirt with black tights, and black boots that came up to her calves.

Kayden walked out with Ava. "Time to head out!" he said.

We followed him and stood by the road, grinning, waiting to see where he led us.

"Hop on!"

Ava and I looked at the motorcycle that Kayden was scooching up toward the front on. Then we both cracked up laughing.

"Good one," Ava hooted, slapping my arm, and I shook my head as we both kept howling.

"Ahhhh," I let out a sigh of laughter. I really needed that.

"You're going to get in trouble if the owner of that thing comes out!" I told him.

"This is mine. When I have a large tour group, I take the bus. There is only three of us, so we take motorcycle."

Oh, good lord. He was serious.

"How old is that thing?" Ava asked.

"No need to worry, ladies, I do this all the time. The weather is fine, and we will be able to maneuver in traffic better to get to see more. Now, hop on," he said, patting the seat behind him.

Ava and I vied for the placement of getting to sit behind him with arms around his waist. She was larger than me, but I could be scrappy when I had to be. I may have grabbed a chunk of her hair to get first placement behind Adonis. It was well worth the fight, too. Suddenly, I didn't think this was such a bad idea.

"Don't forget we share a room, and you fall asleep before I do," Ava leaned in, whispering in my ear.

I shrugged my shoulders. Still worth it.

Kayden wasn't kidding when he said the motorcycle could help us maneuver in traffic. He was going in between cars, zipping into lanes that weren't really lanes, and we were getting many nasty stares and some unwelcome hand gestures as we sped to our first destination.

At one point, Ava groaned, "I'm glad I'm in this position. I may throw up!"

Trouble was, I believed her. This sort of thing had happened before with us—this would *not* be our first hurling incident.

"Ah, we have arrived at our first stop: the elegant, historic Zona Colonial, which is now called Ciudad Colonial. We begin with a bit of history."

We hopped off the bike, landing on the cobblestones with shaky legs. We tried to regain our equilibrium before we began the tour of this beautiful historic region.

"This is the main attraction of Santo Domingo," Kayden led us to a spot like an actor moving to their marker, then turned to us to begin.

"As well it should be, as this is the first settlement that was established off the east bank of the Ozama River in the fifteenth century. The Spaniards used this settlement in the 1600's to gain influence in the Americas and used that to conquer the Caribbean Islands." Kayden gestured with one of his hands like Vanna White, showcasing the architecture around us.

"In 1655, there was an invasion by English officers, but Spanish troops impeded it. At this time, the defensive wall was modified after the siege and expanded. The nineteenth and twentieth centuries is when the city started to expand beyond its boundaries to the beautiful coastal area you see today. The Ciudad Colonial remains the main attraction," Kayden ended his speech by handing us each a pamphlet with pictures, and more information. "Later, I want both of you to watch the merengue dance. The real deal—I'll take you to the real Santo Domingo streets. Plus, we must try to visit Los Tres Ojos!" He smiled at us. "Now, I will let you both walk around and explore as it is intended to be seen. I will meet you back here in say an hour's time. Or would you like longer?"

"That's fine, thank you!" I said.

"You are very welcome, my blonde beauty," Kayden reached for my hand, and, as he bent to kiss it, he momentarily paused to look up into my eyes and smile seductively at me. With that, he left.

"Hello, Jolie, we have an hour. Are you going to stand there and live out your sex fantasy until he returns?"

"Maybe," I mumbled like a zombie. Ava grabbed me and jerked me out of my romance novel.

We walked around alone, taking in the sheer beauty of the exterior buildings all in pale yellow, white, and stone.

"Look, it's the statue of Christopher Columbus!" Ava bellowed, pulling me into the center of the square where the bronze man stood, pointing toward the sea, on a pedestal inscribed with allegorical symbols.

"It says here that he is the one who explored and colonized the Dominican Republic in 1492. He named it La Hispaniola," I read from the pamphlet.

"I did not know this," Ava said, getting a selfie of

herself in front of the statue.

"Here, let me get one of you," I said.

Ava looked up at the statue and mimicked his stance, pointing toward the sea. At the moment I took the picture, a pigeon flew up and landed on her pointing finger. Ava screamed bloody murder and turned to run, colliding with the statue, bouncing off, and landing on her behind.

"Are you okay?" I asked while working hard to suppress a giggle. I couldn't help it; I snapped another picture.

"You jerk!" she yelled at me. Other tourists were giggling too, and a few started to film the scene.

"Shhhh, I'm sorry. I don't mean to laugh. Seriously, are you hurt?"

"No, not that it matters," Ava said, pushing herself from the ground and wiping the dirt off of her behind. "None of these people nor you would help me as you're all too busy with your cameras!"

Some tourists had the decency to look ashamed and put their phones in their pockets and walked away. Some kept filming and laughing. Ava stomped toward these unlucky few.

"Hey, turn it off!" Ava bellowed, charging toward a young couple.

"Calm down, miss. You are fine. We don't often get such humor in this square," the man said.

"Do you work here?" I asked.

"Some days. We are Renaissance couple, as you Americans say," said the drop-dead gorgeous woman. She had bleach-blonde hair with her natural black showing at the roots. She had a full-body leotard on, which was an odd look, but flattering to her figure. She wore lots of make-up even though I doubt she needed it. The man she was with was equally handsome.

"I've never used that expression," Ava snarled. She still was not happy with these people.

"So, you two are lesbians?" leotard lady asked.

Ava's body tightened. I wasn't sure the lady meant any harm, but Ava was already ramped up.

"Yes," I said, grabbing Ava's hand. "She and I have been friends since childhood, but it grew into more. We are planning marriage soon." Once I got started, I couldn't stop making things up. "In the States, we are champion merengue dancers. It's why we're visiting here. We want to see the culture of the dance." I finished my tale and squeezed Ava's hand.

Ava stared at me like I had lost my mind. Kayden had just mentioned this dance. We were trying to enjoy ourselves today before dealing with more family drama. I wanted to be a champion dancing couple. What possibly could be the harm of that?

"You are kidding, no?" the blonde beauty asked.

"No, she's not kidding," Ava insisted, playing along. "I know you wouldn't believe it to see me fall back there, but I am the one who leads. Lesbian merengue is very popular in the States." I nodded.

The couple was suddenly extremely friendly. The man wrote something on a small paper and handed it to us. "You must come here at this time. You will love it, I promise," he said, gesturing towards the piece of paper.

"Sure," I said, tucking it in my short's pocket. We weren't going, but they didn't need to know that.

We headed back to meet Kayden.

Next, Kayden drove us to the National Palace to show us what he called the Dominican version of the White House. Then, knowing how much American women love to shop, he took us to the Blue Mall, which was huge, gorgeous, and filled with different styles clothes, jewelry, purses, and shoes. Ava may have spent a little too much money there. Kayden wanted to take us to the Los Tres Ojos Park to view the underground caves, but we didn't have time to do that and watch the dancing.

Our last stop of the day involved getting to see, first-hand, the main dance of the Dominican Republic—the merengue. As he drove, he pulled over and stopped on a side street where we heard loud music and saw locals in the street moving to the beat. The crowd was not large, only a few men and women enjoying themselves.

This seemed to be the real Santo Domingo of the people, not for the tourists. The buildings were old and dilapidated, the streets broken, and the sidewalks cracked. The men and women wore threadbare clothing that seemed a little too big for them but was held up with belts.

What stood out most to me was the sheer joy that exuded from their spirits as they danced in the street. Kayden led us up to them, and the men and women reached for us to join them, showing us how to sway quickly left to right, cross our legs at our ankles, and spin back around. The men and women coupled up, pointing so that Ava and I couple up as well. They showed us that one should lead, and that was Ava—she held my right hand with left hand around my waist, and our hips were to move right to left. Next, they tried to show us how to move to an open position so we could circle each other while still holding hands. Somehow, we ended up bumping heads.

"May I?" Kayden asked, and Ava passed me to him. Another man took Ava and began spinning her around.

"Follow my lead, Jolie," Kayden whispered in my ear. I didn't like that I had tingles and shivers moving up and down my body. It was easy to follow his lead as he was strong and held me tight as he moved my body with his. The temperature seemed to climb fifty degrees, and sweat beaded up on my head. My face felt flush.

He pulled back to show me the correct way to do the open position, holding onto my hands and moving me around in small circular steps. He held eye-contact with an intensity that made my insides melt like snow in the oven.

We were pulled out of our merengue zone when Ava tumbled over the curb and fell to the ground.

Again, I tried not to laugh. Ava was not as upset this time as the women ran to help her to her feet, and no one was grabbing a phone to video it. I swallowed my laughter.

"Now we go see champions in action," Kayden said, reaching for my hand.

We entered a ballroom that had a huge ceiling with art from the colonial period covering it. The walls were a deep burgundy, and a crowd was gathering around the dance floor. Many people seemed to know Kayden and allowed us to move to the front of the group.

Kayden put a hand on the small of my back, whispering in my ear, "This will be exciting. These performances are seductive, with strong sexual energy. These are the great merengue dancers of the Dominican Republic. You will not forget this."

"You came!" Blonde leotard lady squealed, appearing out of the crowd. She and her man friend moved from the dance floor to Ava and me. Ava immediately looked angry having recently been offended by this flamboyant couple. They had changed into their performance costumes. Hers was silver with spaghetti straps, and tapered down to a thong, leaving nearly nothing to the imagination. There was not much to it. She had on nude pantyhose with pointed heels. The man wore skintight black pants, dancer shoes, with a button-down black shirt open to reveal his tanned chest. He had purple sequins on the shirt. If these were their costumes, what were they wearing earlier? Casual daywear? What did this woman wear to the grocery store?

"We never believed you would show," the man said.

"Oh, you can believe it!" Ava crossed her arms.

"Raphael, take this one, I take the blonde," Silver Thong said, pulling me away. I looked back at Kayden, who looked as confused as I was.

Fifteen minutes later, I was wearing a similar outfit to Silver Thong, whose name turned out to be Penelope. I was attempting to pull the string out of my nether regions, but it wasn't coming out. My hair had been teased as big as it could get, and I had three layers of makeup on. The heels were a no-go. I told Penelope she needed to get me flats, and she wasn't happy about it. I assumed we were getting dressed up as a gag and was waiting to see what Ava looked like. It would make for a funny picture.

Penelope grabbed me, and we met Raphael and Ava in the hallway. Ava's costume was similar to Raphael's. We both giggled.

"I need to get our cameras so we can get a shot of this before we change," I said, moving toward where we stored my tote.

"No time, we must go," Penelope said.

"Go where?" I asked as they both dragged us out to the dance floor.

"Wait, what is happening here?" Ava asked, trying to use her weight to pull back, but Raphael was too strong.

People were cheering and chanting, "Merengue! Merengue!"

"You two stand here. Since this is our country, we will start. You watch, then it's your turn, yes? We compete! Renee, Lucas, you stay with them until we are done," Raphael demanded.

Renee and Lucas looked to be frightening security guards that glared at us. I looked across the dance floor, and Kayden looked amused, but he was whistling at me and clapping.

Fast-paced rhythm filled the air, creating heightened energy in the room as Raphael led Penelope to the center of the floor, showing off her perfect-ten body. Next, he led her close to where we stood left of stage and then took a starting position. She lifted her right leg and he picked her up straight into the air. Before they began, Penelope screamed a warrior cry, the music blared, and her body weight fell behind his back as he held her ankle with one hand, quickly grabbing her arm to pull her up in front of him. She landed flawlessly, then he held her hips, and they moved in perfect beat to the music. The two grasped hands and their hips began driving the dance in an ultra-fast unison.

The next several minutes were a whirl of spins, lifts where Penelope went airborne, twists that wrapped her around his body like she was a boa constrictor, and twirls that dominated every inch of that stage. At one point, Raphael stopped as Penelope dropped into a squat, and he held one of her hands as she spun so fast I swear I caught the tailwind of her turns. The crowd began roaring and chanting, "*Hur-a-cán, hur-a-cán!*"

"What does that mean?" I asked Ava.

"Hurricane."

"We don't have to do that, right?"

It all happened so fast; I could barely keep the moves straight. There was some unison side-by-side hip moves. The one thing I picked up was that Penelope every so often would be let go of with one hand while Raphael held the other, and she would point to the audience and smile, and they went nuts for it. I caught myself clapping and screaming for them. It was so impressive.

Then, the music stopped, people cheered and screamed, and the couple extended their arms, gesturing for Ava and me to take the floor.

I gulped. "Did you watch what Raphael did?" I asked.

She didn't answer me. I elbowed her and looked at her sideways.

Ava shook her head.

"We can do this. Maybe not that good. But, we did this in the street. We watched. It won't be that bad," I said, as the Hulks pushed us toward the floor.

"I hate you so much, Jolie," she hissed. "I swear once we are back in Ohio and all, and I do mean *all* of this is behind us, I am selling my house, my part of the restaurant, and you are out of my life for good."

I looked at her nervously. Had I finally gone too far?

Ava put on a huge smile, grabbed my hand, and led me center stage. I sashayed my behind, allowing her to lead me as the crowd screamed for more. I put on a dazzling smile, holding my other hand in the air with my hand down and head high in the air. Kayden did a wolf whistle, and others began to mimic in turn.

Ava then turned to walk me back to where Raphael and Penelope stood in our previous places. They glared at us, daring us to beat them. Ava glared right back. Me, well, I cowered a bit.

Ava held her hand for me to put my foot in it. I looked at her like she was insane.

"Put your foot in my hand. You wanted to do this. Do it!" she growled.

"You are not lifting me straight into the air, Ava. No way!"

"Give me your foot," she reached down to grab my foot, and I pulled away as the music began to blare.

"Stop it!" I panicked.

Since she couldn't get to my feet, Ava opted for squatting and wrapping her arms around my lower calves, grunting as she stood up and lifted me in the air. I was so taken aback momentarily, I screamed. The audience thought my yell was similar to

Penelope's war cry, and they screamed with me. My eyes widened in terror as Ava heaved me awkwardly over her own shoulder, and I crashed to the floor.

The entire audience gasped as I sat up. I tried to slip into a sitting pose that looked graceful, and move my body around like Penelope had, but the thong rose, and my butt cheeks chafed on the wooden floor. That was going to leave a mark.

Ava grabbed my arms and jerked me to my feet. She mouthed, "Side-by-side!"

I followed suit, and we began moving our arms and elbows like a mix between runners and boxers, not in unison at all. People began to boo at us.

"Keep going," Ava said as she grabbed my waist and right hand and moved me around the dance floor to the beat of the music.

I worked to shake my hips as much as I could, but my rump was burning from the floor-burn. Ava was taking gigantic steps to try and use the entire stage as Raphael and Penelope did.

I felt like we may be hitting a groove. The one thing I did a lot was point at the audience and smile. No one cheered for me, though.

Ava leaned into me and said, "Next I'm going to stop, you bend at the waist, I'll grab your hand and spin you while you are bent down like they did."

I started to protest, but she stopped, and I bent, Ava grabbed my hand, and I did a pathetic toddler turn around maybe a half turn before I stood and said, "I'm done!"

The music stopped mid-song. The room was silent as people gawked. Many were videoing this, of course. I would have been.

Surprisingly, Raphael and Penelope graciously came out to us and clapped and turned to the audience, saying, "Please thank our American friends for the Benny Hill-type performance for us all!"

What was up with Benny Hill?

The crowd roared.

Ava and I hung our heads in embarrassment and moved to the back to put our clothes on in shame. We had let our country down.

Kayden kindly took us to dinner at a local casino after our complete and utter humiliation.

"You were both fabulous! I had no idea you had such a sense of humor!"

"Oh yeah, we can't get enough comedy," I said.

We were seated with our drinks and delicious, fresh crab legs and lobster before us when a woman in a bright red dress walked up and slapped Kayden in his face.

Ava and I were mid-fork-to-mouth and stopped in disbelief.

She then turned on Ava and me and yelled, "Good luck with this guy!" and stormed off.

"What was that all about?" I asked.

"She was a tourist who did not have enough to pay for the day," he explained. "She wanted to pay me in other ways, but I am not that kind of guy."

"Seems like you maybe should have taken her up on it," Ava said.

"Why you say that?" Kayden asked as though nothing had happened. He began tearing into his lobster.

"One, she's hot, so why not? Two, you wouldn't have gotten slapped."

"This is true."

Kayden finished his meal before us and told us to take our time. He wanted to get some gambling in.

"I hope he doesn't have a gambling problem," Ava said.

"It's probably just recreational." I took another buttery bite of lobster.

"I suppose it is possible. Although I get the feeling there is more to this guy that what we see," mused Ava, still watching him over my shoulder. Then her eyebrows shot up. "Um, speaking of..." She pointed, and I turned around, still chewing.

Kayden was arguing with the roulette dealer as two huge guards were coming up behind him.

Chapter Four

Kayden was in a hurry to get Ava and me back to our hotel room after all the violent displays at the casino. We had peppered him with questions, but he refused to tell us what the issue was; instead, he went on a lengthy spiel about how Santo Domingo was known for being the industrial, commercial, and financial center of the country. Kayden then wished us goodnight and departed. We were exhausted after the events of the day and fell asleep almost immediately.

"AREN'T YOU TWO SUPPOSED TO BE HELPING THE MARTINEZ FAMILY?" screeched a familiar voice.

Why was Grandma Opal in my hotel room in Santo Domingo? I opened my eyes groggily.

"ARE YOU JUST GOING TO SLEEP THE DAY AWAY?"

"Huh?" I said, sitting up in bed and squinting, trying to understand if this was real or a nightmare. Oh, she was on my phone. I fell asleep with my phone in my hand and must have picked up on her video call in my sleep.

I looked at the clock. We had slept late. Yikes.

"We had a big day yesterday." I yawned.

"Your hair shows it."

"I was sleeping!" I protested.

All of a sudden, I could no longer see Grandma. The video was being jerked all around, causing me to feel seasick.

"What are you doing? Stop that!"

"Shhhh!" Grandma's face was smushed into the phone.

I jerked my head back. I think this was Grandma's first-ever video call.

"Don't shush me, woman!"

"What is going on?" Ava growled from her bed.

"Grandma Opal is doing her first-ever video call," I said.

"Hey, Mama Opal!" Ava's voice changed to a sugar-coated tone.

"Hey, sweetheart! Wow, you just waking up?" Grandma asked.

"Yeah, guess we slept in this morning."

"Well, you need to do that every so often. You look good, girl. How do you wake up looking so amazing?" Grandma asked Ava.

I rolled my eyes, not realizing I had shifted the phone back to my face.

"That's very unattractive, Jolie," Grandma said.

"Grandma, is everything okay with the restaurant?" Change of topic, please.

"Oh yeah, that is nothing for the two of you to concern yourself with. The Tucker crew has it covered."

"What about the cats?"

"Don't worry, Jolie. We are all visiting them daily. Multiple times a day, even. That Sammy Jr. still won't come out for me, your mom, or your aunt, but supposedly he loves that grandson of mine."

Well, that was progress, Grandma calling Tink her grandson.

"So, what's up with the call?"

"Well, that's what I was trying to show you before you started being rude!"

Yeah, *I* was being rude.

"I didn't see anything but a bunch of movement."

"Well, I can't let him know what I'm doing!"

"Who?"

"Mick."

So, they are on a first-name basis now.

"Where are you?"

"I'm having lunch at M&M's Italian Restaurant. Look!" She angled the phone and said, "Tell me when you can see okay. I'm acting like I'm leaning on the table looking at it."

She continued to angle the phone in different positions until I saw them. Ava crawled into bed next to me.

"Stop!" I yelled.

"Shhhh," Ava and Grandma hissed simultaneously.

"I doubt they can hear me!"

"Who is he with?" Ava asked, leaning in.

"It's Lydia," I snarled. It felt like a punch to my gut, but I would have to come to terms with it. I took a breath. No one likes to think about their ex with someone else, but if this made him happy...go for it, I guess!

Meiser was seated across from her, and there were candles lit on the table. She leaned across at one point and brushed his cheek.

Ava sat up straight, "Oh no, this is not good!"

"What, it's nothing," I said unconvincingly. Still trying to wrap my head around Meiser possibly with another girl.

Next, Lydia got up, and Meiser stood and grabbed a cane before stumbling to move toward her to help her from her chair.

A cane?

Lydia reached up, touched his chest, kissed his cheek, then walked away.

"See what I mean," Grandma Opal panicked. "You need to get everything sorted out with Ava's family and get back here ASAP!"

"Mama, she can go back now," piped up Ava. "I can handle things down here."

"I'm not going anywhere. What is wrong with the two of you? He told me he doesn't want to be with me. We've barely talked the last four months. He has a right to move on, as do I."

"Who are you moving on with?" Grandma barked.

"Adonis," Ava said.

"Huh?" Grandma asked, squinting her eyes at me.

"Kayden." I shot daggers with my eyes at Ava.

"Who is that?"

"He's this super-hot Greek-god-looking guy who was our tour guide yesterday. He has the hots for your granddaughter, and she wants him to get naked."

"Hey, do you remember what you said to me at the merengue competition? Well, do that!" I said.

Ava stuck her tongue out at me.

"Sleeping in? Taking tours? A merengue competition? Hold on, are you two on vacation? Is there a crisis with Ava's family or not? Were you lying?" Grandma looked downright furious.

"No one lied, Mama," Ava said.

"What exactly is going on with your family, anyway? Patty said she didn't get all the details."

"And it's going to stay that way," Ava said, getting out of bed, going into the bathroom, and closing the door.

I swear I was going to kick her a—

"Who is Adonis?"

"A guy named Kayden."

"Well?"

"Grandma, I have to go." I disconnected and crawled back under the covers.

🫐

As we finished getting dressed, Ava asked, "So, are you upset about Meiser and Lydia?"

"We don't know for sure that there *is* a Meiser and Lydia." I sighed. "Although, in all honesty, I would rather see him with anyone in Leavensport than her."

I was trying to use some tools I learned in therapy, but I felt a bit like I was being split in half.

My normal reaction to this would be to feel incredibly jealous, think hateful and spiteful thoughts about Lydia, and want to punish Meiser for it. Jolie *after* therapy sessions *wants* to be an adult who can process all of this, be okay with it, and realize he is the one who did not want to be with me. He has every right to move on with whomever he wants. I still hadn't decided whether to listen to the angel or the demon on my shoulders.

"I know."

Lydia and I had a history of being frenemies—more enemies than not. It wouldn't surprise me if she were doing this on purpose.

My phone rang again.

"I hope Grandma isn't following Lydia and Meiser around town," Ava said.

"It's Kayden!" I said excitedly.

"What? When did you give him your number?"

"Last night, now shush!"

I cleared my throat, "Hello," I said breezily.

"Well, hello, Miss Merengue Champion!"

I laughed.

"Free for lunch with me?" he asked.

"Today?"

"Yes, problem?"

"Um, hold on a minute," I muted the phone and turned to Ava. "What's the plan for this afternoon?"

"I'm heading to the parents to see if anything new has developed. Why?"

"He wants to take me to lunch." I smiled with my whole face.

"Are you doing this because of Meiser and

Lydia?"

"Yes, that is the driving force of everything I do," I said sarcastically. "Do you need me today?"

"Go be with Adonis."

"I'd love to. What should I wear?"

"Something sexy if you must be a bad girl, BUT I say again, be careful of that one, Jolie. He's too good-looking, and there's more to him."

"I plan to be reckless today."

"It *is* about Meiser," Ava mumbled.

I pretended I didn't hear her.

I wasn't dressed sexy, so I acted more slutty than normal to make up for it. I have a hot little black dress back home, but I didn't see a reason to bring it with me. I ended up wearing a pin-striped pants suit.

Kayden knew all the best places to eat in the city, and the lunch was spectacular. We lounged in the patio seating on a beautiful, balmy day sipping sangria and eating tapas, but yet again, a *different* woman walked up to slap Kayden. It was lovely, but he seemed a bit off like the day at the beach when he got a call.

I looked at him in amazement. "Women *really* hate you!"

"Yeah." He took another bite of his salad like nothing had happened.

"You seem used to this behavior."

"I mean, I don't enjoy it, but I guess you get used to it after a while." Kayden looked a tad guilty.

"I feel like you are trouble." I tried to look stern, but it just came off flirty.

"And you like trouble?" He grinned, reaching and rubbing my hand.

"Not concerned I'll slap you?"

"If only," he sighed blissfully.

"Normally, I'd be afraid of this behavior. Today, I feel careless."

"You *look* like dessert."

"Do I?"

"Let's head out of here and go someplace more cozy."

The place he took me to wasn't just *a place*. It was a mansion.

"There is no way you can afford this place on a tour guide's salary," I said, turning slowly to take it all in.

Kayden grabbed me around the waist and spun me around. "How do you know it is my place? You said you liked trouble, right? Well, I happen to know for a fact that the people who own this home are out of town. Now, let me give you a tour."

He led me up the stairs. I took a moment to wonder if he was kidding or not. He led me to the bedroom where I saw a picture of him and a man. "You lied."

"I'm good at that. Bad boy," he began unbuttoning my jacket, laying it on a chair in the corner of the room. Then he moved to my blouse, kissing me softly on my face, neck, and chest.

I took a deep breath and pulled back. "So, what else have you lied about?"

He fell onto the bed and patted the space next to him.

It was tempting. All I could think of was kissing

Meiser. He and I had never fully been together. Did I really want to sleep with this man? I shook the thought from my head. Why couldn't I be an irresponsible woman for once?

"Go ahead, ask me anything," Kayden said, sitting up on the bed and pulling me by the waist to him.

"Why did those women slap you? I don't appreciate men who lie."

"No woman does."

Looking down at him, I raised my eyebrows with a straight-lipped expression.

"Okay, maybe I can be a bit of a Casanova from time to time. But—"

I pulled away, "Don't say it."

"What?" he grinned.

"I'm different."

"You are."

"Right." I thought back to Lydia placing her hand on Meiser's chest. "I don't care." I leaned into him, pushing him back on the bed and lying on him.

Things were heating up in Kayden's bed when the doorbell rang. I was halfway undressed at this point.

"I'm sorry. You stay here. I need to get this." Kayden kissed me and grabbed a robe. Again, his face looked panic-stricken. Ava had a point; he was too good to be true.

I laid back, thinking about what I was doing. I was supposed to be here supporting Ava and helping her family in any way I could. This was helping no one. Well, maybe me a little. I heard yelling downstairs and hurriedly dressed, purposely not putting my shoes on so I could sneak down the steps without being heard.

Easing down each marble step, I overheard Kayden threatening someone.

"You better not even think of touching a hair on her head," Kayden yelled.

I heard a loud slam and ran down the steps. Kayden had shoved the man into the door that stood open when two men ran from a downstairs room and pulled Kayden off the stranger.

Words were exchanged, the man left, and the two men looked up at me.

I held a hand up with a small wave. The two men disappeared in the same room they came from without a word.

Kayden turned and ran to me, putting his arm around me. I realized I was shaking.

"It's okay, it's okay. C'mon. Everything is fine. No big deal."

Kayden led me to the little table in the kitchen nook and pulled out a chair, then poured two cups of coffee. I didn't have the heart to tell him I didn't drink the stuff.

"Thanks," I said, taking the cup. "What was that about?"

"It was about life."

"So, you are not just a tour guide, are you?" I asked, smiling and gesturing at the beauty that surrounded us.

"I give tours because I love it. This is my family's home. We all live here. It's big enough, no?" He grinned.

"I've only seen part of it. Were those guys

relatives?"

"They are security for the family. You just saw why firsthand."

"But why are people...randomly attacking you?"

"Let's just leave it at...sometimes people don't like us just because we have money." He shrugged his shoulders. "We got used to it. And also hired security." He smiled sheepishly. "I guess annoying people until they want to hit us runs in the family."

My brain played a mental montage of Kayden getting slapped by various women. "Ah, a bad boy, as you said. I'd like to know what you meant about not touching a hair on her head. Another one of your women friends?"

"This is a private matter with my family that I cannot discuss with you. And that is truth."

"Okay, for now, I guess," I said, thinking back to Ava's warning.

"See, I don't lie all the time." He took a big gulp of coffee. "You need cream or sugar?"

"Mmmm . . . I'm a tea drinker."

"You like chocolate?"

I laughed.

"I take that as a yes. You wait. You are in for a treat."

Kayden began working on something in the kitchen.

I stood and took a few steps to the sliding glass door. Looking out, I saw three palm trees side by side. There was a breeze moving through, and the tree in the middle swayed, brushing against the tree on the right. Even though the tree on the left stood close to the others, it seemed isolated. I felt a little like that.

"Come here, you," Kayden said, putting down a large, steaming mug of something that smelled chocolatey and had whipped cream melting into it.

"Wow, this looks like something I will drink," I said, sitting back down and taking a big whiff of my hot beverage.

"This is not just any hot cocoa. This is my family's special cocoa. You try," he said, pushing the mug toward me.

I blew on it and sipped. There was an explosion of deep, rich, toasted nut combined with a fruity wine flavor. It was amazing. I had never tasted anything like it before.

"It's incredible," I said, knowing that word did it no justice. "It tastes like red wine, but there's also a toasty or roasted nut taste in it."

"I'll send some home with you. It's a special dark chocolate blend, and you have good taste buds. There are toasted nuts and dried cranberries in it to give it that wine taste."

"I see why your family lives here."

"We do well with the business. We do a lot of export and make the majority of our money there."

"Ava's family is in the export business, too. They deal in gold."

"Ah, she is a Martinez."

"You know them?"

"I don't know them but know of them. Everyone knows the Martinez family. I'm sure they have heard of my family, the Rodriguezes, too."

"You're probably right," I said, taking a large drink.

"You've heard of the movie *Pirates of the Caribbean*?"

"Of course."

"There is a history of pirates in the Dominican Republic."

I chuckled, "Are you saying the Martinez family comes from pirates, and that is why they are in the gold trade?"

"Some say this is true, but there is no proof of that," Kayden said, circling his coffee cup with his thumb. "The family we know for sure that were pirates is a family known as the Perezes. They eventually got mixed up in the mob."

"I don't see Thiago Martinez wearing a skull and bones hat with a patch over one eye," I said testily.

"The pirates turned into the Mafia. Gold has been found buried in different places around Santo Domingo. This is why some people spread rumors that the Martinezes could be mixed up in this."

It seemed too coincidental to me that less than four months ago, Meiser was telling me his family was mixed up in the Mafia. Now this. How was I supposed to discuss this with Ava?

Chapter Five

"So, nothing happened, Miss Reckless?"

"A little hot and heavy making out, but that was about it." I recounted the events of the previous day to Ava. "You were right. He is too good-looking. There was no way he is Mr. Perfect. So, how did it go with your family?"

"Ugh, let's put it this way—I'd rather be back in the ballroom being booed and hissed at." Ava rolled her eyes.

"That good, huh?"

Ava stood up and rubbed both hands up and down over her face. "Jolie, there is so much more going on than blackmail. Someone drained all the money from the business account. Papa and Mama had already found out about it, but somehow Lolly wasn't aware."

"Does she do finances for the company?"

"Data entry," Ava mimicked her sister's voice. "That's all she says: 'data entry.' Theo works there, too. I wouldn't be surprised at all if that little weasel is involved. I feel like they all know something that

I don't. I ask questions, but they just start talking in circles."

I bit my tongue, wondering if I should bring up possible Mafia ties.

"Do you know how much money the people want?" I used air quotes around 'the people' as to not be gender-specific.

"Fifty thousand dollars," Ava said. "Papa tells me not to use our money, but his accounts are drained. I want to ask him what he can do in two weeks' time to come up with that kind of money on his own, but I know better!"

I did a low whistle. "That's a ton of money for anyone, especially if your accounts have been drained."

"I know. I keep going back to why are the blackmailer's giving us two full weeks and why on Valentine's Day? There has to be a reason—a connection to that."

I reached for the laptop that I had charging on the little table by the hotel window. "Let's note that on our I Spy Slides."

"Yeah, and we've both taken a lot of pictures while we've been here. I'm thinking it couldn't hurt to create a collage and put them on a slide in case any of them could be of use later. I know it's a long shot, but seeing that I'm completely in the dark, I have no way of knowing what is relevant to our investigation and what isn't."

I stopped typing, looked up at Ava, and grinned.

"What?"

"You sound like a PI with the 'our investigation.'"

"Oh yeah, I'm a boss babe!"

"So, are you going to be helping to get all the funds together?"

"I'm getting ready to call Denise to see what all I need to do to have it wired. I'm hoping she can tell me what I need to do when I get to the bank. I mean, will they give me a bag for all that cash? I have no clue. I've never laid eyes on that much money. It will be all I can do to resist going straight to the Blue Mall for a shopping spree!"

"Are you having the full fifty grand wired?"

"If she can do it, then yes. I'm sure Papa has some to contribute, and you know how he is. He will die making sure he pays us back."

"Knowing him, he will want to calculate and pay us interest," I said, knowing the pride of Thiago Martinez.

"It makes me sick to my stomach to think about borrowing against the restaurant to give to these, these—"

"Dirtbags!" I rang out.

"Good one."

"Ugh, Meiser just texted me."

"At least it wasn't a video call," Ava was applying mascara while flitting her eyeball back to where I sat, glaring at my phone.

"He's probably with Lydia," I said, feeling dark anger surface and trying to tame it to a cool blue breeze as Tabitha has told me to do.

"I was thinking that!" Ava put the mascara down.

"Thanks," I said, typing back a message.

"What did he text?"

"He's asking how things are going here. He said

it's not the same there without me."

My fingers began angrily, pushing the buttons on my phone's keyboard.

"Uh, oh, I know that furious typing. That is not good. Don't text angry!"

"Too late. It's sent."

"What'd you say?"

I read from my phone, "Fine."

"That's it?"

"Yep."

"You looked to be furiously typing longer than 'fine.'"

"I deleted the rest. There were too many curse words."

"Oh, I took my niece and nephews to La Franny's Bistro yesterday while you were doing lord-knows-what with Adonis. I set it up so we can go there today for a Dominican cooking demo. You better get ready."

🔵

"What did Denise say?" Ava and I were in an Uber on our way to La Bistro Franny. I still couldn't get over riding in a car on the coast, looking over the vast blue waters. How did drama of any kind exist in paradise?

"They can wire the money, but if I take that much out in cash, then it alerts the government, and we go on some list. I didn't understand it all. It will be a whole other issue dealing with taxes on taking that much out too."

"We'll figure it out. One thing at a time."

We arrived at Franny and Yoselin's. They had extra help in front so they could show us some things in the back. I was amazed at how tiny their kitchen was. The four of us could barely move back there. It gave me a whole new perspective on our kitchen at Cast Iron Creations.

"So, what are we making?" I asked, squeezing past Ava to get up close to Yoselin for the demonstration. Ava's eyes widened two times their normal size as I scooted by, letting me know nonverbally how tiny this kitchen was.

"*La Bandera*," Yoselin said. "The flag. It is called this because we set up the rice and beans to look like our flag. The meat is supposed to represent the blue. We always add a side salad of lettuce and tomatoes."

"It's a staple in our country," Franny said.

"What is it?" Ava asked.

"Rice, beans, and meat are a must to make this dish, and I add plantains as well. These are all used in almost every meal here. This is a variation on it," Yoselin said. "This is my father's recipe."

"My mama used to do most of the cooking, but she hasn't of late," Ava said.

"Yeah, because your family has a cook!" I exclaimed.

Ava shoved me playfully, which caused me to slam into a shelf where pans crashed to the ground. Everyone flinched and looked at me.

"I'm so sorry!" I said, bending to pick them up. There was a pamphlet sticking out from under the oven. "Oh, looks like someone dropped this."

I went to hand the pamphlet to Franny and noticed it was the exact pamphlet Kayden had given us the day before, only this one had a note written in marker on the front. Being a Nosey Nelly, I went to read the note, but Yoselin snatched it away and stuck it in her back pocket.

"You take tours of your own town?" I teased.

"Nah, Kayden recommends three different restaurants to tourist. We are the number one restaurant," Yoselin said with pride.

No wonder he wanted to meet here.

"So, you ladies are from the States, but here visiting family?" Franny asked, switching topics.

"Her family, not mine," I smiled and pointed at Ava. "The Martinezes, they live over by–"

"*Dios Mio*," Yoselin said, looking at Franny, panic-stricken.

She turned, and I saw that the pamphlet was about to fall out of her back pocket. I took that opportunity to snatch it, and stuffed it in my tote.

"What?" Ava asked, surprised by the reaction to her last name.

Franny's eyes darted back and forth. "Oh, uh— nothing. I mean, we've heard their name. Who hasn't? Yeah, I bet you do have a cook."

"*I* don't have a cook," Ava said.

"Sure you do," I lightly punched her shoulder and smirking.

Ava rolled her eyes, "No, I don't. My parents do."

"Well, getting back to the recipe, the secret is all in how you prepare the beans," Yoselin said.

"And the rub for the meat," Franny added, squeezing past us quickly. She stopped, facing away from us, and took a deep breath. Then she turned around. Her face was pink, and she seemed upset.

"I'm sorry, I know you came here to get a demo, but we are going to get unusually busy," she said, speaking quickly. "We need to get our lunch special ready. Yoselin can write the recipes down for you to take back." Franny rushed us to the door to the front of the bistro.

"Oh, okay, well, thank you," I said, grabbing my tote and moving out of the kitchen.

Ten minutes later, we were headed toward the Martinez home in an Uber with recipes in tow.

"So," Ava said, looking at me.

"Yeah, that was strange."

"Seemed to be your fault."

"My fault?" I sang out.

"You started nosing around with that pamphlet."

"It had thick black marker on it. It was difficult *not* to look at it. What about Franny after she heard your family's last name?"

"Yeah, I didn't like that at all. But I can't help what my last name is. You can help being a snoop."

"Says the soon-to-be private eye."

"So, what did the note say?"

"I could only make out that there was a long number with dashes in between numbers. It did say 'Do' first, though. I don't know—then a bunch of zeros, then numbers."

"Weird."

When we got to the house, the family was sitting in the living room, quietly conversing. The first thing I did was to slip into the kitchen and reach for a glass, pour in the tea, scooping many tapioca pearls into the drink and garnishing with a wide straw. I needed my bubble tea fix.

"You are going to turn into a bubble head," Lolly said, wandering into the kitchen.

"A what?" I asked while slurping the fruity, creamy tea down—banana-strawberry flavor. Delicious.

"We used to joke about the bubble tea. We'd drink so much, Mama and Papa called us bubble heads," Ava said, laughing.

"What's this?" Lolly asked, picking up the recipes that Franny had started to write down for us before she pushed us out the door.

"We were just at a nice local restaurant. It was so strange. They were going to do a demo for us to walk us through how to make a couple things, but then Jolie got nosey, and they turned weird," Ava said.

"Not just me," I finished my drink. "Franny freaked out when she heard the name Martinez."

Lolly slammed the recipes on the counter and stomped away. I could hear her clomping up the steps.

Ava looked at Theo to see what was wrong. His face had turned beet red.

"Do not bring that name up here," Thiago bellowed.

Sophia ran up the stairs, I assumed to check on her daughter.

"What's going on?" Ava asked.

"Oh! I think I know," I said. "Franny was the one that Theo—"

"I said not to mention that name!" Thiago turned and slammed the door, heading to the patio.

"Nice going," Theo said, striding toward the front door.

"He did *not* just sass us when he is the

adulterer," Ava said, going after Theo.

"Leave it be," I said.

"We need to head back to the hotel and add more to the I Spy Slides, anyway," Ava said.

"Like?"

"We should probably add Franny and Yoselin to our list of suspects, don't you think?"

Chapter Six

Ava and I had spent some time doing some online research to find out what we could about Franny and Yoselin. Santo Domingo was like the States in that everything was now digital, but vague in many respects.

"So, the only thing we got about their families is that they both come from impoverished families, but they obviously pulled themselves out of that to build a successful business," Ava said.

I was adding notes to our slides on the two women. Before the awkwardness at the restaurant yesterday, Ava had snapped some pictures of the four of us together, so I added those to slides.

"I'm not finding a lot online about the financial status of the restaurant," Ava said.

"I doubt we could find out how they got the money to open it."

"That would be good to know. The only thing I got is that the restaurant had a grand re-opening about six months ago."

"I'll try to find something in the news," I said,

switching over to browse the internet.

"I'm going to call Papa and ask where the public records office is. Everything is ambiguous online."

While Ava called Thiago, I tried a few different keywords to find anything on La Franny Bistro. Finally, I got a hit.

"Okay, I just called an Uber to take us to the records office," said Ava. "Did you find anything online?"

"Yes, the restaurant caught fire last year around this time of year. It was a big news story at the time because they believed it to be arson, but they never found the perpetrator."

"Arson?" wondered Ava. "It's such a tiny place. Their food is inexpensive. Why would someone want to burn it down? Even Franny and Yoselin wouldn't make much from insurance off of that place, would they?"

"Depends, that is something else for us to look into."

Ava's phone buzzed. "Oh, Uber's here."

We zoomed across town to the records office.

"Are you sure this is the right place?" Ava demanded.

"This is it," Uber man said.

It was a broken-down, neon-yellow, single-wide trailer. We approached slowly. Ambling in, we were ignored by a man behind the counter. His hair was dark, oily, and slicked back, and he wore extra-large, black-rimmed glasses, a plaid, short-sleeved shirt with a pocket protector with unmatched, plaid shorts, white socks with sandals behind a counter. The only reason we saw his feet is because they were planted on the counter as he watched a tiny, black-and-white TV program with squiggly lines running through the screen.

Ava cleared her throat.

The man looked up, annoyed, then taking us in, he hastily stood, tucked in his shirt, pushed his hair back, and did the hand to mouth blow to check his breath.

"Well, hello, ladies. What can I do for you today?" He must have stood too fast because he grimaced and rubbed his lower back, groaning quietly.

"Hi there, we'd like to look through some records, please," I said.

"Tell me what you need, and I can get them for you, no problem."

"Any issue with us telling you what business we are looking for, and then you allow us to sneak back there and snoop around on our own?" Ava asked in an overly-sugary voice.

"Oh, well, I'm not supposed to do that."

"Say, what's your name?" Ava asked coquettishly.

"Randy."

"Wow, Randy. LOVE that name. It suits you perfectly." Ava reached out and walked two fingers slowly up his chest, leaning over the counter to show her cleavage.

Randy took the bait and hook.

"So, Randy," Ava drawled out his name while batting her eyelashes, "I completely understand rules and all. We co-own a restaurant in the States—policies and rules are important. There are times when they are made to be broken, though.

Now, my *familia* lives here. I need to locate only a little information on a local restaurant called La Franny Bistro. Any way at all that you can look the other way while we pop back there to take a quick looksy around?"

I was trying so hard not to allow my mouth to drop open. The only time I saw the flirtatious side of Ava was when she was with Delilah.

"Well, as you say, there are rules for a reason. Not everything back there is open to the public," Randy looked left to right to make a point, "but there is no one here for another hour or so. I will be drinking my stale coffee and finishing my show as if no one is here."

Ava's smile spread from her cheeks to her eyes. "Randy, you are a *bad boy*, aren't you?"

"From time to time."

"Mmm...me likey!"

We hurried around the counter and through the open door to the back room, where my mouth fell open. "This place is a MESS!"

There were boxes and folders everywhere, with papers hanging out of them. There was what looked like a two-decade-old copy machine with footprints and shoe scuff marks all over it from people kicking it.

Ava groaned. "I'm not sure we will be able to find anything in this mess—definitely not in less than an hour. Should I ask Randy for help?"

"I mean, you put on quite the show out there. I'm sure he would be more than willing to do anything for you."

"I'm torn. He's given us full access. What if he gets antsy and asks us to leave?"

"Let's start looking on our own, and if we don't find anything in fifteen minutes, then you can work your magic. You start on that side, and I'll start here."

Ava and I began trying to figure out the organizational system of the boxes. The one nice thing is it was easy enough to find the restaurant section. Once I found it, Ava moved to the end of the restaurant boxes, and I started at the beginning as we dug in. The bad thing was that there was no apparent filing system—not alphabetical, not numerical...

"How's it going back here?" Randy sauntered back, rubbing his middle pouch to let us know it was his eating time.

"This is so nice," Ava said. "We are looking for some information on our friend's restaurant La Franny Bistro. You have done such a fine job—we found the restaurant section in no time!" I snorted but managed to cover it with a loud cough.

"Thanks, honey, I try to keep it all organized. Neither of you are looking in the right box, though. La Franny Bistro is in this box here," Randy swaggered to the end of the aisle of shelves and grabbed a box that read TO BE DETERMINED.

"What does that mean?" I asked.

Randy looked at Ava while answering my question, "This is the box of restaurants that were flagged for having defaulted on loans within a three-year period. Not paying taxes or defaulting on loans or something like that."

"Great, thanks so much, Randy." Ava sidled up to him to grab the folder from his dirty hands.

Randy peeked inside the folder, and his face

changed. "Oh, um, yeah, this is one of those things that are not for public eyes."

He had gone pale, and his hands shook as he put the folder away in the box and walked up front with it.

Ava and I looked at each other in a panic. We needed to distract him and fast.

"Randy, I noticed when you first stood that you looked like you have some back pain," I said, concerned.

"I sit all day, every day. It's my lower back." He put the box down and rubbed his back. "It's been getting worse lately."

"Ava has the *exact same* problems with her back," I rattled on, thinking on my feet. "She does a *lot* of yoga to relieve it." Randy glanced over at Ava, probably imagining her doing yoga. "She swears by handstands. Yep, handstands. To stretch out the lower back. You know, the decompression. Hey, Ava! You could take Randy up front and show him how to properly do a handstand to help his back pain."

Ava's lips spread apart slightly, her face froze, and her eyes went to slits as she said, "Yeah, sure, Randy, you won't believe how much this can help and how quickly you get relief."

I grinned as he forgot the box as the two headed up front. Ava had taken him around the counter by the window, allowing me to go through the box of information without fear of him seeing me.

I hurriedly looked and found some documentation on La Franny's Bistro. Rather than read it all, I grabbed my phone from my large brown leather tote and began frantically taking pictures of each document to get out of there as soon as possible.

When I finished and walked up front, Ava was standing on her hands with her feet resting against the front window. Her loose top had fallen to her face showing her lace-covered bosoms. Randy appeared to have forgotten about his pain with the show in front of him.

"Did you try yet, Randy?" I asked.

"Um, no, I am learning a lot from her...demonstration." He blushed.

Ava flipped back onto her feet, scowling at me.

"I try now," Randy said. "You help?"

"Sure," Ava and I moved to Randy as he put his hands on the ground and shifted his weight so that his legs moved to the window. We held his legs up.

"How's that?" Ava asked, looking to me, shrugging her shoulders, and giving a half-grin.

"Oh, wow, I never would have thought I could do this."

"You're doing great. Does your back hurt at all?" I asked.

"No pain."

"Well, thanks for all your help. Our Uber just pulled up, so bye!" Ava said.

We ran out of the building, leaving Randy upside down.

Back at the Martinez home, Carmen offered to show us how to prepare the *La Bandera* since we didn't get to learn from Franny and Yoselin. Ava wasn't as interested as I was, so she spent time playing with her niece and nephews. I found out that there were many ways to create the beans and the sofrito rub for the meat. Carmen explained that rice and beans were a staple in all meals in the Dominican and how one changed up the rub mixture, and the preparation of the beans made all the difference. She showed me a variety of ways to do so. She also gave me great notes on where to find the best online videos that I could watch to help me make the dish when I was back in the States.

The best part was sitting down to get to enjoy the fruits of our labor. Carmen had opted to combine chicken stock, tomato paste, adobo seasoning, and parsley with some finely cut onions, celery, and carrots to make the red beans. I had never been a big bean fanatic, but now I planned to explore more.

After we finished our meal, I helped Carmen clean up while Ava went upstairs to talk to her father in his office.

Carmen and I were clearing dishes when I saw Rafi manhandling Lolly on the patio. He grabbed her upper arm, squeezing it hard, causing Lolly to wince. I saw her hands curl into a claw position. I moved toward her, but he let go. I realized the door was cracked open, and I moved behind the wall in the kitchen by the sink to see if I could hear what was going on with those two.

"You won't do this again to me. I will not let you ruin me!" Rafi bellowed.

Carmen came in with more dishes, and I smiled at her, pretending to be cleaning.

"I've done nothing to you. How do you not get that!" Lolly yelled.

Ava and Thiago moved into the kitchen. Carmen lowered her head to stay out of it.

I moved with Ava through the door in time to see

Lolly try to storm away only for Rafi to grab her elbow. She turned and shoved him hard, nearly knocking him onto the floor; instead he hit the side of the wall, and then she flew out of the patio door as it slammed behind her.

"What did you do?" Ava yelled at Rafi.

"Mind your own business, you big buffoon!" he roared, stomping away and leaving us all gaping after him in confusion and anger.

Back in our room at La Casa Renaissance hotel, I asked Ava if she knew anything about Rafi and Lolly.

"Nothing at all."

"I'm going to add that little dramatic scene to our slides," I said.

"Wait, you think Rafi and my sister are involved in blackmailing my father?" Ava gasped, recoiling away from me. Then she leaned over the table and pointed in my face, "My sister would never do anything to hurt my family!"

I sat back with hands up. "I'm not saying she would. I'm saying there's a question of what's going on with her and Rafi. Theo has already proven to be a liar and a cheater. I'm looking at Rafi. It's just that your sister was the one in the argument with him."

Ava's vexation made me leery of bringing up anything Kayden had said about her family possibly having ties to the Dominican Mafia. I wanted to add that piece of information to the slides. Actually, I had thought about looking into links between Meiser's family and this situation. It was too much of a coincidence. Even though I could easily make a document that Ava didn't know about, I felt like I was cheating on her. Maybe I was being too paranoid. There was mafia everywhere. But, in less than six months, I had run into two mafia families? Is it a coincidence, or are they somehow connected?

"What did you find out about the bistro?"

I was happy for the change in subject. "I haven't had a chance to look at the documents yet."

"You stole the documents?"

"No, I took pictures, and I just uploaded them to a slide," I said beginning to read through them.

Ava leaned on the chair I was sitting in so she could read over my shoulder.

"What? The Perez family is how Franny and Yoselin financed their restaurant."

"Why do I recognize that name? Or wait, was that the name Papa mentioned before?" Ava asked scratching her head.

"Kayden mentioned them. Pirates turned Mafia."

"Yikes, I wonder if they had something to do with the arson?"

"Well, I read the news story about the arson. The timing works out for when the girls started to lose money. I'd assume that would mean they got behind on payments."

"Why would this information be in a government building?"

"Randy looked white as a ghost when he looked in that file. I wonder if it had to do with seeing the Perez name?"

"Make a note that a higher official could be involved. Doesn't seem smart to leave this information out unless you aren't worried about it."

"Typically, where there is a lot of money and

power, crime follows."

"I wonder if Theo ties into this somehow since he was with Franny?" Ava asked.

"Could be. I'm also going to note that Kayden recommends their restaurant. Is he somehow connected to all of this?"

"Good point. Do you think it's odd that this is the second time in less than six months we are dealing with a mafia group?" Ava bit her lip.

"Yeah, believe me, I've thought of that a few times."

"Make a new slide and list everyone associated with any mafia in any way so far."

"Um, okay," I said, doing as Ava instructed.

I pulled pictures in where I could onto the page and listed names out: Milano, Cardinal/Nestle? Martinez? Perez.

"Whoa, whoa, whoa," Ava started.

"*I* don't think it. Kayden mentioned to me everyone knows your family. Something about gold being buried all around Santo Domingo and some people think your family is tied into the mob," I spit out as fast as I could.

Ava reached over me to the mouse to highlight and delete her family's name.

"I'm sorry," I whispered. "I *swear* I don't think your family is involved. It's just that your family is in trouble. The date is looming overhead. We are no closer to figuring this out. I don't want to miss something."

Ava's eyes brimmed with tears as she typed 'Martinez?' back into the list. "I know we are sharing a room, but do you mind going to the lobby for a bit? I need a few minutes alone."

"I understand," I said, grabbing my tote and shoving my laptop into it.

I went down to the bar and got a glass of red wine, sitting in a corner booth. I grabbed my therapy journal and began writing.

- *Meiser and Lydia*
- *Tucker family secrets—Uncle, aunt, multiple cousins I've never known about*
- *Meiser's real last name is Milano—his family is involved with the Sicilian Mafia.*
- *I swear I saw someone digging in the fields for sale near Meiser's restaurant. Were my eyes playing tricks on me?*
- *Buried treasure—pirates.*
- *Buried gold—Martinez family? Perez family?*
- *Dominican pirates now Dominican Mafia? Connection to Leavensport? Martinez family.*
- *Cardinal/Nestle—mob connections? Tri-City—urban sprawl—acquiring Leavensport land.*
- *Martinez family secrets?*
- *Meiser's brother was mayor of Tri-City trying to purchase Leavensport land— Meiser purchases land for restaurant.*
- *What's buried in Leavensport?*

I looked up as the waitress asked if I'd like another glass of wine. I had gone to the bar for my first glass.

"No, I'm fine. Um, is this your standard uniform here?"

"Yes," the waitress said, dropping her voice and looking at me like I was insane.

"Do you know the name of that lady taking off her apron and leaving?" I asked, pointing across the dimly lit bar.

"I'm sorry. She is new. She was in training with management today. She seemed too friendly with management if you ask me."

She looked very familiar, but it was too dark to be sure who it was.

Chapter Seven

I had snuck back up to our room around one a.m. after a few too many glasses of vino. Ava was asleep when I crawled into my bed.

The next morning, I was awoken again by a video call—this time from my Aunt Fern.

"Huh?"

"Are you doing nothing but sleeping there? Your grandma told me you were in bed when she contacted you, girlie!" Aunt Fern looked to have a new, tightly curled, grayish perm with a large floral scarf around her neck.

"Where are you?"

"I'm at the mall doing a little shopping. Just got a new do, and wanted to get something snazzy. Trying to keep up with Mom."

"What? Why do you need to keep up with Grandma? Is she there with you? Will you hold the phone still? I'm getting sick. You know you can all call or text instead, right?"

"I'm walking to get my steps in. Nah, Mom isn't

here. She's got herself a new man, so I'm going to try to wrangle me a man, too."

"Grandma's dating!?"

Ava sat straight up in bed, stood carefully on the mattress, then proceeded to hop over to my bed, losing her balance and falling on top of me.

"OW!" I groaned.

"Sorry." Ava apologized, distractedly. "But who are you talking to?" I aimed the screen at her.

"Hey, girl," Aunt Fern hooted.

"What up, Fernie? You are looking fine as wine!"

"Right?" Aunt Fern said, putting a hand up to pat her perm.

"Why is the phone shaking so much?" Ava looked at me.

"Give me a break, you two—" My phone tumbled all around. "It's how you video-talk! We're hip!"

"Um, I don't think so," I said, slowly sitting up and rubbing my side.

"Who is Mama Opal dating?" Ava asked.

"Thomas Costello," Aunt Fern grinned.

"You know, the guy who called the police on her for stealing his plastic grocery bags for me to use as liners for the trash cans for the cats' litter boxes? Apparently, that is their version of flirting."

"You mean Tom," Ava said.

"*She* calls him Thomas. He says she's the only one allowed to."

"It must be love," Ava took both her hands to shape a heart from her two index fingers and two thumbs at Aunt Fern, who confirmed with a head shake.

"How's things going there?" I asked.

"Everything is fine. Business is good, all shifts are covered for the next two weeks, with people offering to help beyond that. The cats are getting spoiled—more so than normal. I'm not sure you will be able to get rid of Tink when you return."

"Hopefully, he doesn't get too comfortable," I couldn't help saying.

"Yes, that sister of mine says you've been a bit of a turd lately. Attitude and all."

"Wonder where I get it from."

"True, you get it honestly." Fern's voice got a serious edge to it. "Your mother loves you, and you know that. We all do. You and I joke a lot, but there's something I need to say, and I need you to hear me."

Ava quietly stood, grabbed some clothes, and moved to the bathroom.

"Aunt Fern, I don't—"

"I don't care what you want or don't want right now. You are going to sit there and listen. The Tucker family—well, your grandfather and his relations and your grandmother's relations come from the Kentucky mountains. Lots of kids in their families. Not many got a lot of education. Back then, in that area, the oldest had to help tend to the young uns. Over the years, all the things they went through caused a lot of tension and drama within the family."

"Not closeness?"

"Yes and no. Anyways, Jolie, there's a history and that history carries down to our little unit of the family. No time for all of that on a video chat, is there? But one day, we'll all sit down and hash it out. The thing to remember is that we all love you. We all love each other, even if it doesn't seem that way."

"Okay, Aunt Fern. I'll remember that," I said, squinting at the screen. "Hey, Aunt Fern?"

"Yeah, darlin'."

"Is that Lydia behind you coming out of the garden area? What is it she has?"

"Looks like she's buyin' a shovel of some sort."

"Weird timing seeing it's winter there."

"Well, now, you and Lydia have always had your issues. Gotta run! Got another call coming in."

With that, she was gone.

Ava was still showering. I looked back at my last awkward text to Meiser. Was he seeing Lydia? Maybe he was having an MS flare-up and she was helping him as a nurse. Ugh, Lydia would hate me for my next thought. She was purchasing a shovel; I saw someone burying something in the field—I think! I can hear her now; *you blame me for everything!* And she was right. If something untoward was going on, I admit that my mind jumps to her right away.

Uh, I needed to get over this Lydia thing. Yet another reason I need to figure out what I want for my future and go after it. The question is, do I take some time to be strong on my own or move forward? Something to talk to Tabitha about when I return home.

I tapped the reply button on the Meiser conversation. *Sorry for being so abrupt with you before. We're here to help Ava's family, but there's been a lot of downtime. How's your health?*

I stared at the phone for a minute before hitting

'send.' I tapped the button, then got up to get dressed for the day ahead.

●

Ava and I were in the hotel restaurant taking advantage of the breakfast buffet when she got a call from Lolly.

"You're where?" Ava asked into her phone.

I chomped on my bacon, looking speculative.

"Put the plate down," Ava said, calling for an Uber.

"What's up?"

"Lolly's in jail."

●

Speeding into the jail, we ran into Thiago, Sophia, Theo, and Rafi. I wasn't sure why Rafi had to be here, but he was. They were releasing Lolly on bail that I heard Rafi had paid for.

"What happened?" Sophia asked, hugging her daughter.

"Let's walk outside. I need fresh air," Lolly said.

"You have GOT to be kidding me!" Franny stomped up to Lolly. Franny's face was swollen with a huge black eye. I took a step back.

Theo looked ready to vomit.

"What happened to you?" Ava exclaimed.

"Like you and your family don't know!" Franny yelled, huffing heavily.

"Hey, it's one thing for you to blame me for your misfortune. But you do not point your adulteress finger at my family, Franny!" Lolly took two large steps to Franny, getting in her face.

"This is what she did yesterday afternoon in our restaurant, except she had a knife in her hand and threatened Franny," Yoselin stepped in front of her friend to fend off Lolly.

"What are you talking about?" Thiago took a step in front of his daughter.

"Come on, we all know about me and Theo. I get jumped last night making a deposit after she threatens me with a knife? You're going to tell me you people had nothing to do with it? I'm sure little Miss Perfect wouldn't get her hands dirty, but I wouldn't put it past her to hire one of your mob thugs to rough me up," Franny's eyes welled up with tears.

"What the heck are you on?" bellowed Ava in a blind rage. "My family is not involved with no mob. Lolly wouldn't hire anyone to hurt you, nor would she do it herself. Do you think this piece of crap is worth a night in jail?" Ava pointed to Theo.

Theo's face turned bright red. His brother, Rafi, looked amused.

There was someone else who connected the Martinez family to the mob. I grew up spending so much time with Thiago, Sophia, and Lolly, I didn't want to believe it was possible. Maybe they were being threatened again? That's the only way any of this made any sense to me.

I looked down and saw my mom was trying to video-call me. I hit ignore. I couldn't deal with any more family drama right then.

The whole getting-Lolly-out-of-jail business in Santo Domingo took *way* longer than I thought it would. Not that I had a ton of experience with it in the States. After all the family awkwardness, Ava and I split from her family to have a late lunch, early dinner.

Ava and I stress-ate until our hearts were content, then had a quiet ride back to the hotel later that evening.

"I know what you are thinking, and you are wrong," Ava said.

"You don't know what I'm thinking."

"Franny mentioned the mob. You're thinking about what Kayden said about my family."

"Didn't cross my mind." It did, but I couldn't bear to tell Ava that.

"They are both wrong. There is no way my father would get involved with them. He was willing to give up shares of a company that his ancestors created in order to stay *out* of the mob's control and *protect* our family. He gave up a lot, money included, to stay out of it."

"I know that. I grew up with your family. Do you think I want to believe any of this?"

"So, you do?"

"I don't know. I don't want to. Could someone have threatened them? What did you mean about giving shares to someone?"

"Papa's best friend was Ron Rene Sanchez. Ron Rene was legit but was on friendly terms with the mob and he had connections to the police as well. He offered to buy shares of the company so that he could take over for Papa so he could move Mama away. They were ready to start a family, but Papa was too worried to do it here. The Mafia was moving into all of the major trades in Santo Domingo. Obviously, gold was huge. Now, my family refused to stoop to mobster-like tactics in business, but it was a different story when it came to the Perez family—and yeah, it was the Perez name Papa mentioned before, I asked. The two families were enemies, and there are stories of the Martinezes being ruthless when they felt a Perez had wronged them. This dates way back."

"Right, Kayden covered some of that. The Perez family was supposedly pirating that stolen gold and burying it around Santo Domingo. Eventually, they became the local mob."

"Right. I don't know the timeline with this, but the Perez family had an opposing company that rivaled Martinez Nuggets. My great-grandfather wanted a monopoly and put them out of business. My understanding was it was all legal, though."

"So, the Sanchez family took the majority of shares from your father?"

"Fifty-one percent, giving Ron Rene the power to make decisions. My father still was invested, and Ron Rene kept him in the loop. Ron Rene died last year. Somehow he had calmed the waters with the mob before he died, and the shares went back to my father. This is why they moved back. Lolly and I were grown, no reason not to go back.

"Could any of this tie into what's going on with Lolly, Theo, and Franny?"

"I know I harp on Lolly being too perfect for her own good all the time. But I'm telling you I *know* she is not involved." Ava was heating up.

I had opened our I Spy Slides and added what happened to Franny. I also added the information Ava had just shared about her family's history. I wanted to start from the beginning, going through the pictures, reading the notes over again.

"There's so much going on. It's like there are connections, and then there are other things where I can't make a real connection, but they seem important," I said.

"I know. The mob, I feel like there are connections there. Is it us? Are we reading too much into everything?"

"We have to, right? You're the PI."

"I'm not officially yet. But yeah, you're right. We have to note it all. The difficult part of investigating is working through what's smoke and mirrors and what is real."

"How do we do that?"

"Look for patterns."

"Okay, would you agree that gold seems to be at the heart of all of this?"

"Yes."

"Many people are screaming 'mob.' The theme of the mob is a pattern, not just here but in Leavensport, too. I think we should look into that when we get back," I said.

"One thing at a time. Gold, Mafia, blackmail, money."

"Family?" I asked.

"What do you mean?"

"Family feuds dating back generations. A family stepping in to help—the Sanchez family helping yours. There is something secretive going on with Lolly and Rafi. I'm not saying anything bad," I hurried to get that last part in as Ava got defensive again, "but you have seen it too."

"I need to talk to her." Ava's brow furrowed. "And I need you to stop making accusations!"

"I know this is personal for you, Ava, but we have to look at all sides of it. This could be your family's financial future!"

"I need some space." She grabbed her purse.

I was staring at the picture of Ava fallen on the ground in front of Christopher Columbus. I noticed something off.

"No, you stay here. I'll leave."

I got into my Uber and asked the driver to take me to Parque Colon in the Zona Colonial.

"Why is such a sexy thing like you going out to a tourist spot alone at night in Santo Domingo?"

I felt my skin crawl as he stared too long in the rearview mirror. I had thought about asking him to stay and wait while I investigated, but now I was thinking I'd be better off calling another driver than dealing with this creepy dude.

"I think I left something there," I said, grabbing my phone and pretending to text something in the hope that he would leave me alone.

As we pulled up, he said, "Let me park, and I'll walk you over. It's dark and I'm afraid the security lights aren't what they used to be."

"No need," I grabbed some money and shoved it at him.

I went to take my seatbelt off when, suddenly, it felt like an earthquake had hit. The car lunged, and I heard loud metal grinding as my body jerked, causing my neck to pop.

Something had crashed into the Uber. The impact was hard enough that the driver's airbag deployed. Luckily, I hadn't taken my seatbelt off yet. Unfortunately, the driver was turned around to take the money. His body rammed into the windshield.

I pulled my seatbelt off, pushed the door open, and stumbled to the ground. My tote had been between me and the door as I was reaching for money. When I opened the door, it fell out, scattering the contents of the bag.

I reached for my phone but felt a foot hit my back, knocking me into the ground. I felt like all the breath inside of me deflated from my soul.

I tried to look up but could only make out a hooded figure. I tried to roll over, and the figure shoved me back. My hand fell on this little gadget my Aunt Fern had bought for Ava and me. It's a self-defense claw. I hold it in my hand, and little divets go in between my fingers. When I squeeze it, metal claws come out—like Catwoman or Wolverine.

The attacker came at me, and I squeezed and swung at his face. I must have hit him because I heard a scream. It was a man's voice.

He recovered from my strike and came at me again. I tried to crawl away.

I cowered, preparing for the worst. I knew I was too battered by the impact to fight back at this point. The Uber driver must have hit our attacker, because the assaulter fell to the ground by me. I looked over, momentarily catching his eyes. Familiar. Then he got up and ran.

"Are you okay?" It was the Uber driver, bending over me. He had his phone out. "Do you need ambulance?"

"No, I just need to catch my breath. Are you okay?"

"A bit shaken. The impact knocked me out for a bit. When I came to, your hooded attacker was getting ready to take you out."

"Thank you for helping me," I said sincerely. He smiled.

I guess I shouldn't judge a book by its cover.

Chapter Eight

The police had come and gone last night. One good thing was because we were in a public area, there were security cameras everywhere. The police took both of our statements, and said they'd get access to the video to see if they could find out information. They told me they'd call me to follow up.

I was feeling bruised and banged up again. I was going to insist the Uber driver leave. Who knows what would have happened if he hadn't been there?

"I can't believe you did that," Ava exclaimed.

"You are not giving me grief for getting attacked, are you?" I asked incredulously.

"Yeah, Jolie, I am giving you crap. You and I left things awkward. I thought you were going to the lobby to work and give me some space. I didn't know you were going out in the middle of the night to risk dying. Imagine how I would have felt for the rest of my life if that had happened!"

"That's true, I really should have thought ahead about all the what if's when I went out investigating in Santo Domingo to help YOUR family, in order to

be sure, you would be as pleased as punch!" I
declared sarcastically.

"That's all I'm sayin'!"

As if I wasn't already ready to go into an empty
field, throw my body to the ground and scream as
loud as I could into the festering dirt of my life, I
saw that Meiser was video calling me. Great.

"You need to answer that," Ava said, leaning
over me and hitting 'accept.'

Lord, please give me strength *not* to strangle my
best friend.

I plastered on a smile, "Hello."

"Is anything broken?" My mother must have
shoved Meiser out of the way to get a look at me.

"Yes, Mom, I'm fine. Aren't I always?" I asked,
thinking my nine lives were about up.

"That right there is the point, young lady. We
should not be having this conversation, because
twenty-four-year-old women shouldn't have their
lives put in jeopardy multiple times in one year."

"She's right, once a year is MORE than enough,"
Ava laughed standing behind me waving to my
mom.

"Ava Marie Martinez, this is no laughing matter.
Your family is in trouble. You two have been in
harm's way enough. Now I have to hear from my
nephew that you are taking private investigator
courses. You best not think you are getting Jolie
Lynn involved in that. Better yet, I helped raise you
too—as of now, those classes are *over*!"

Oh, good Lord, my mom was throwing out
middle names left and right. Ava and I looked at
each other, and she took off. "Chicken!" I hissed
after her.

"Mother," I began.

"Do not 'Mother' me, Miss Thing."

"Okay, take a breath, Mom. I'm fine. How did you find out?"

"Sophia knows the mother code. She called me last night to let me know what was going on and that you are fine. I noticed you or Ava didn't have the decency to call me. Mick had to be the one to help me with a video call so I could see for myself. Plus, he's very worried, Jolie. And he misses you. When are you both coming home?"

"Stop it!" My voice raised two octaves to get her to listen. "My relationship with Mick is none of your business. Whether or not Ava takes PI courses is none of your business. If we want to shut down the restaurant and start our own PI firm, then that is what we will do. I have to hear all this crap about our sweet little family, and we'll work through all the strife of the past from Aunt Fern and Grandma. Well, maybe, but all of you need to learn boundaries!"

Wow, that felt AMAZING! Better than finding a good empty field to scream in. While I had been able to stand up for myself in the past with my family, I was *never* able to follow through with reasons why I was upset and solutions. This was a big accomplishment for me to stand up to my mom.

My mom's lips went straight, and her eyes turned to slits. I waited, staring her down. I could feel Ava breathing next to me out of line of sight of the video. Coward! The next thing that happened shocked me.

"You are an adult. Take care of yourself. I'll see you when you get back. Love you," and she gave the phone to Meiser.

My head slowly turned to Ava, who had peeked outside the bathroom door when she heard me yell, while both our mouths hung open.

"That was a bit harsh, wasn't it?" Meiser asked.

"She's always been a helicopter mom," I said.

"No, I mean you."

My head jerked back in self-defense, "Me? What did I do or say that was so wrong? Sticking up for myself, being an adult."

"She's just worried about you. She's a mom. It's what moms do." He looked good. His thick, wavy brown hair was messed up like he just woke up.

"Just because you and your mom don't have a strong relationship, don't project your inadequacies on me." As soon as I said it, I wanted to take it back. He looked like I punched him in the gut. He stared off in the distance with pain in his big brown eyes.

"Oh, no. I'm so sorry, Mick. I'm tired and in pain. My emotions have been all over the place," I was trying to justify my bad behavior.

"It's fine. You're right anyway. Hey, I'm glad you aren't hurt too bad. I do miss you. Take care. I gotta head out." He disconnected, not letting me get a word in.

I jerked my head and hand toward Ava who had now come out to support me, "Don't even think of saying anything." Tears welled up in my eyes.

"I'm going to go shower," she said, squeezing my shoulder.

I grabbed a pair of cut-off sweats and a cute Santo Domingo cat tee and put them on with my comfy tennis shoes and headed out to clear my head.

When we first arrived, we had gone to the beach, and I noticed some old walls near the water. I decided to go for a walk down by the beach. I took my shoes off the second I hit the sand. Ava had told me these walls were known as Fortaleza Ozama. It was an area of fortresses with old architecture. I slipped my shoes back on as I walked up the steps to follow the path around the walls and old building.

These walls seemed to be talking to me. Every time I felt I achieved something—took a step forward, I felt like the next move was two steps back. My entire life was made of fortresses like these, made of the strongest human-made material—neglect, rejection, and despair. I didn't want these things to affect me the way they have. I'd love to overcome and be stronger for it. But everything that has happened to me has shaped me too. I put the walls up to protect myself, as these fortresses were built to protect the port entrance of Santo Domingo from seaborne enemies.

I don't think of myself as a mean person. At least, I don't want to come off as coarse. But here's the thing, I've been hiding and overcompensating for as long as I can remember. I'm afraid to be hurt, but I'm also afraid to stand up for myself. It's become a routine—feels set in stone. Thoughts chased themselves around my head as I walked along, tracing my fingers along the roughness of the stone wall.

Patterns. Ava said follow the patterns to help figure out an investigation. It's the same with past trauma. Father leaves, comes back, leaves, comes back—doesn't even need or want to see me when he's back. New, real man in my life—I fight it. When I realize my stepdad is the real deal man I can trust, my world changed. It grew, and I could see light. Then, he gets cancer, and he dies. I'm dating Keith, and I go back into myself again.

More patterns. My mom, grandma, aunts, and uncles overcompensate for what I've lost. They rally around me. They are great in every single way. As I become an adult, I can't breathe anymore because my brain and my heart are playing emotional ping-pong—yet, they aren't playing the same game, and it makes me nauseous and feel like I'm crazy at times. But my family, they are following a pattern and routine they created.

Balance. That is what I need to find and work toward moving forward. I need to find my strength within me first. Then I figure out what I want and need in my life and go after it. I'm getting there.

I shook myself out of my thoughts and looked around. I had come into the square, Parque Colon. I had gone to the statue because when I looked at the photograph of Ava with the statue, I noticed in the picture that a stone on the cathedral wall behind it was moved, and something was hanging out of it. I never got to see what it was, but when I walked behind the statue, whatever was hanging out was gone. I felt the stones looking to find the spot in the picture and noticed one was fake, but nothing was in it. I decided to go inside to investigate more. I noticed again as I felt along the wall that one of the stones felt fake. Lighter, kind of, like the one outside. I felt around. It was dark inside the cathedral. I grabbed my phone and put the flashlight on looking over the wall I had just felt. It all looked the same.

I closed my eyes, walking backward, slowly feeling the stones. Eventually, I felt a difference in texture. One spot wasn't coarse or rough, but too smooth, and perfect human-made material, like plastic. I stopped, turned the flashlight on, and felt around the stone. They all looked alike, but this one was definitely not natural. I tried pushing and nothing. Next, I tried to jam my fingernails into the crevices and pull but nothing. I put my hand in the center and slid left, right, down, then when I slid my hand upwards, I felt a catch—like a latch was there. I held the flashlight close to the top of the fake stone and pushed inward enough to see a tiny latch, and I grabbed a pen from my tote and took the end and pushed up, releasing the front of the stone.

Inside was one old, rusty tin can with no label. I pulled it out but heard other people walking in, so I threw it in my tote to investigate later.

Walking outside of the fort, I noticed I had a voicemail from Ava. She left me a message saying the money was ready and asked me to meet her at the bank. I texted her that I was on my way.

●

When I arrived at the bank, Ava was sitting in a cubicle, fidgeting nervously, waiting on the money.

"Hey," I said, sitting next to her.

"Where did you go this time?"

"I went to the fortresses to walk around and think."

A man in a tailored business suit walked out carrying a briefcase. I found myself beginning to squirm nervously in my seat, too. Ava and I were only able to start our business with a loan. We both worked through high school to save money for a down payment on the building we wanted. Cast Iron Creations had been a kid's dream of "playing restaurant" as five-year-olds turned to planning for the future as ten-year-olds—yeah, we were unusual kids. As kids, we did chores around our homes to make money and had the Pig Out Cast Iron Creations Piggy Bank to put our allowances in for our future restaurant. As adults, we simplified the title to remove the Pig Out. Point being, we've worked most of our lives saving to get a down payment in order to get a loan on our restaurant. Both of our families helped us understand at an early age what we would need to do if we really wanted it to happen. We were fortunate. The Martinez family had run businesses, and my grandma and Aunt Fern and Aunt Ellie were cast iron recipe geniuses.

We'd never seen a large sum of money before. So, when the banker opened a case of wrapped stacks of hundred dollar bills and we both saw how many packets lay there, well, I imagined our faces were similar to seeing a dead body. Shock.

"I will need you to sign some paperwork. We will fax some of this back to your primary banking institution in the States. Some are for tax purposes between our two countries. Please sign where you see the X's."

"Okay." Both Ava and I had to sign since we were both on the loan papers.

"Do you have something to put the cash in?" the banker asked.

Ava and I looked blankly at each other.

"Can't we take that case?" Ava asked.

"This is the property of the bank."

"I have my tote and this beach bag I took on my walk," I said, holding up the 'Beach Bum' beach bag with a cartoon cat on it.

We shoved the money into the bottom of the beach bag, putting my large brimmed hat and sunscreen on top of it.

Plodding out of the bank with the weight of the money on my arm, I noticed the chunky cat from Franny's limping along the sidewalk. "Hey, little guy."

He limped up to me.

"Oh my gosh! It looks like he's been shot in the leg," I said, horrified.

"Hold on, I'm calling Mama to ask where the nearest vet is," Ava said, then made a scrunched-up face, angrily snapping her fingers at me and pointing to the ground. A bundle of one hundred dollar bills had fallen to the sidewalk. *Oh, crap!*

My arms reached forward, snatching up the money. I mouthed *sorry* and scooped up the little orange and white cat in my arms. At this point, I was lugging my huge brown leather purse crossed over my body, the beach bag, and now this fluff-a-muffin.

Ava got off the phone and relieved me of the beach bag. "Give me that before you start handing out hundreds to everyone in Santo Domingo!"

"Sorry!"

"There's supposed to be a vet center right down the road from here." Ava looked around.

"There it is," I said, seeing a picture of a dog and cat hugging on a sign.

"You take the cat in to get it checked out. Tell them we will come back to pick it up later. I'll wait here."

"No way, you have fifty grand in that bag. You

come with me!"

Ava and I lugged our heavy baggage of money and cat into the veterinarian office. I gave the receptionist the story of the stray and my contact information to call me when they found out what was wrong.

"Listen, little man–they are going to take good care of you here! I will figure something out for you so you don't have to live on the streets. I promise," I kissed him on his head and rubbed his neck as he purred. Then, we headed back to the hotel to put the money in a secure place.

My phone rang as we were strolling into the hotel. It was the police telling me that they couldn't make out anything from the video from the attack the other night.

"Who was that?" Ava asked, opening the hotel safe and stuffing the beach bag full of money into it.

"The police. They said they viewed the footage from the night of the attack, but there wasn't enough security lighting to get an identity of the attacker."

"That sucks!"

"Tell me about it. Do you know if there are cameras most places and if they record twenty-four seven?"

"Many public places have them now. Most businesses that make a decent amount of money will privately pay for security cameras. Why?"

"That could prove to be helpful later," I said, thinking back to the waitress that looked familiar and that my attacker's eyes were familiar to me, too.

"Let's take a nap before we head over to my

family's for dinner."

Close to an hour later, Ava and I woke to her phone ringing.

"What!" Ava was always grumpy when she woke up.

Her face turned to ash, and I saw her hand shake slightly. I jumped out of my bed and ran to hers. She put it on speaker.

"----Four days until the money is due or you, your friend, and your family will be very sorry."

"I have it. We have the money now," Ava started, then realized she was talking to a distorted recording when the phone clicked off.

"Did they say anything before you put it on speaker?" I grabbed the laptop to add the day, time, and what we just heard to our I Spy Slides.

"Only 'Count Down,' it was all distorted, but you heard me try to interrupt them and it kept going. I'm pretty sure that was a recording."

"Yeah," I said. I was starting to think this whole thing was much more personal than I had originally thought.

Chapter Nine

When we arrived at the Martinez home, the front door was locked, and no matter how much Ava knocked or rang the bell, no one came to answer the door.

"Let's go around back. I know where Papa leaves a spare key in the shed if we can't find anyone."

As we came around the side of the enormous house, we heard yelling in the back. Ava had ducked behind some bushes right next to the house.

"Who is that?" I asked.

"I think it's Rafi and Lolly. I'm not sure if anyone else is there or not."

"You need to leave us be," Lolly pleaded.

"It's not fair! I loved you before he ever noticed you. I'm the one who made sacrifices when our father died. I had to take over being the middleman in your father's business."

"Rafi, I know all of this. I do. I'm sorry I don't feel the same for you. Theo and I are married. We have children. We're in therapy working through issues. We have a past."

"That's only because he stayed in Ohio to pursue you. I had to go back with my papa to help with your family's business. And look at you now, you are still struggling financially. Theo can't help you, but I can!"

"I'd ask Papa for money before you. I'd ask anyone for money before you."

"Yeah, well, good luck with your papa helping you and Theo out with money."

"What is he talking about?" I whispered to Ava. I knew that there was some sort of weird love triangle thing with the brothers and Lolly from back in the day, but I didn't know anything was still going on.

"How would I know?"

"She's your sister!"

"You know we've never been close!" Ava stage whispered loudly.

"Hey! Is that Ava? This is supposed to be our fight, not yours," Lolly said, hands on hips looking around the bushes.

"Oh, sorry, we knocked and rang the doorbell, but no one answered, so we came around back to get the spare key in the shed and heard you two yelling and—" Ava stopped.

"And thought you'd put your new investigative tools of snooping to good use," Rafi spit out.

"Dude, shut up, you are annoying. You heard her. Get over yourself. She's married with kids— plural—*kidzzzz,*" Ava emphasized.

"Ava don't," Lolly said as Rafi stormed off.

"What is he talking about, financial troubles?" Ava asked.

Lolly blanched at Ava's question. "I mean, you know, right?" she stammered. "You're here for...the reason."

"Huh?" Ava shrugged her shoulders.

"I mean, the family. I work for them, right? Theo works for them. We're *all* in trouble right now. I guess except you. You got out."

Lolly turned that around fast. All you need to do to get Ava off-topic is get her angry.

"You have GOT to be kidding me right now! You are now saying that I got out?" Ava went from yelling one second to whispering the next. "Used to be you said I was selfish and didn't know what it meant to stick by family. Now, it's I 'got out.' That's rich, Lolly."

"It's both, Ava. You never thought about what Mama and Papa needed and wanted. Our culture takes pride in taking care of family first," Lolly spit out.

I saw that look in Ava's eyes. She was questioning her intentions. I felt my face flush with ire. "Hey Lolly, you know, your sister is in financial trouble now, too. When your mother called crying about this mess, Ava went into go-mode. She figured out how to borrow against her house, our restaurant, you name it—how to get the money wired, looked into tax issues with taking out large sums. Then, she bought a plane ticket, rearranged other peoples' lives to cover the restaurant, walked away from her relationship. She's got fifty grand waiting to pay to cover your family. So, you tell me how that is not enough for you! She may not live with, near, or work for your family—but when your family needs her, she is there."

I suddenly realized I was in Lolly's face, and my

finger was near her nose. I took a deep breath and stepped back to my spot next to Ava. She had tears in her eyes. Lolly stood frozen, eyes wide. I'd never gone off on her before.

"You have money to give the blackmailers?" Lolly asked.

"No, I don't outright have money. I had to borrow against some capital to get money, and I will have to pay it all back."

Lolly nodded her head and turned and walked away.

"Are you okay?" I asked Ava.

"I don't know what I am right now," Ava whispered, staring after her sister. "But I'm feeling the need to apologize to you."

"Why?"

"You might have been right about my sister being involved."

Chapter Ten

Everyone took a bit of a break from each other for the next twenty-four hours. Ava was hurt by Lolly's comments. I had jumped on the chance to run away from Leavensport, and in turn, I ran from one family dysfunction to another. I felt like a jerk because it was a reassuring feeling to know everyone's family was a mess in one way or another. Seems like common sense, but when I'm living on my own dramatic little stage of the world, it feels like no one else is coo-coo banana pants.

I could tell Ava needed some space to wrap her head around everything. I decided to take a break and first head to the vet's office to check on my little guy, then to La Franny's Bistro to do some work on my laptop and see what the ladies were up to.

I walked in, and the dreamsicle-colored kitty was sitting on the front counter with the receptionist. They had decorated their office with cardboard red and pink hearts, and they had heart-shaped cat and dog treats in a heart-shaped container. I forgot Valentine's Day was approaching quickly.

"I didn't think you'd put him to work so fast," I laughed, walking up and petting him on the head.

"Everyone loves him here. We were going to call you today. His leg isn't broken, but there's a hairline fracture, so the vet put a splint on it to help it heal. He's so friendly, we decided to let him roam around. He's not afraid of the other animals or people and he seems smart enough to know when to stay away from the ones who are frightened."

"I'm so happy he's doing well! Was he fixed already or no?"

"No, he is not."

"Well, let's see. We will be here at least another several days. Is there any way to get him fixed where he can heal here and be able to go on a plane within a week?" What was I doing? These words were just tumbling out of my mouth.

"I'm sure we can work it all out. So, you're hooked, huh?"

"I have cat issues. I have four at home, but I know someone who needs a second," I said.

I took care of what I owed them to date and walked toward the bistro.

On my way there, my fingers automatically found Meiser in my contacts and called.

"How's it going? You in a better mood?" He asked. I could hear the amusement in his voice.

"Haha, I know I was bent the other day with my mom."

"Just a tad."

"Yeah, well, she's got to love me no matter what. Although, I'm not sure I would if I was her."

"Sure, you would. You're not hard to love anyway."

Yikes.

"Well, I'm happy to hear you say that!"

"Oh, boy, I spoke too soon."

"Naw, it's just that Stewart is such a sweet cat. But you are working so much between the station and the restaurant now. He needs a friend."

"He's fine, Jolie."

My phone buzzed, and I pulled it from my ear to look and saw it was Ava trying to call. I hit ignore.

"Is he? Who doesn't want and need a buddy?"

"Stewart doesn't."

"I think he does."

"Okay, why?"

Ava again—ignore.

"There's this cute cat that is a stray here. He's SUPER sweet. Someone shot at him for fun. I took him to the vet, they are getting him fixed, and his leg isn't bad. I'm taking care of it all, but I have four, and you only have one." I rushed through my spiel, which wasn't a very good one since I just thought all this up in the last thirty seconds.

"So, let me get this straight. You take off to Santo Domingo without even a word to me. You put yourself in danger's way yet again, and this time, I'm a couple thousand miles away where I can't see you are okay—"

"Wait, wait, wait, you video called me. You *saw* I was fine!" I protested.

"Are you seriously interrupting me at the same time as begging me for something?"

He had a good point. I fell silent.

"Now you are taking a new cat in, paying to get it all fixed up, and asking me to bring a new cat into my home because you are positive Stewart is lonely. Is this really happening?"

"Yes."

Silence. Lots and lots of silence. I squirmed a bit.

"Okay."

"Really?!?"

"On one condition."

Oh boy! "What's that?"

"When you get back, we need to sit down and talk. I know we have both said this before and done it and end up back in our vicious cycle—"

"I agree to your condition."

More silence.

"Really?!?"

We were both sounding identically incredulous.

"Sure. But this time, we both need to be completely honest. Let's face it—in the past, we were both holding things back from each other. If we're going to figure out where we stand, then we have to be honest with each other."

"Agreed. So, you take care of the cat stuff. I'll tell Stewart he's got a brother coming home."

"Deal. I have to go. I've got a bit of investigating to do."

"Promise me you will be careful."

"I will."

I had walked into the bistro and was standing to the side while finishing my conversation with Meiser. I shoved my phone into my tote and moved to the counter where Franny stood arms crossed over her all-black outfit.

"What have you done with our cat?"

Uh-oh.

"You said it was a stray. Can I get a cup of hot tea, please? Do you have wi-fi in here?"

"It is a stray that hangs around here. We feed it. Others in the lane feed it. It's the community cat. And wi-fi is spotty here. You'd be better off going to the wi-fi café—they are more there for that purpose, and you can always get a signal."

"Wow, I see why business is slow. Your bruises and swelling look better. Still blaming the Martinez family for that?"

"The vet is right down the walkway from us. They come in here. We know you took the cat there. They told us." Franny avoided my question.

"Okay, good. Someone shot at it. It's a stray. I took him in so it could get checked out. There is no chip in it. Yoselin told me you don't even like cats, Franny. I'm giving him a better life inside a home with another sweet cat and a wonderful man. Plus, you know I should be the one being nasty here. You are the one who cheated on my friend's sister. Lolly never asked for that!"

"Men are fools. Complete and utter fools! So easy to get whatever you want from them. Yet, women let men have all the power. It's always been that way. Theo is no exception. And no, actually, I realized Lolly is too much of a coward to fight for her man."

"What did you need from him?"

"None of your business!"

"Did you get it?"

Franny smiled coyly.

"You may want to think twice about how you go about getting what you want. You could end up messing with the wrong person eventually," I warned grimly.

"Thanks, but I don't need advice from a blonde Barbie doll."

It irked me when people made assumptions about me like that. How would Franny like it if I called her a Goth, because she wears all black clothing? I wouldn't do that though, because, first of all, all of the Goth people I've met are the nicest people in the world—well—minus one here. Two, how someone looks makes zero difference in who they are on the inside. Not that I've always known or followed that logic. I was a turd of a kid in elementary school, but I learned it, and work to live by it.

"Okay, leaving now," I stomped out but not without noticing that Yoselin had the door cracked open to the kitchen and was listening intently to our conversation.

I started walking, but I had no idea where to. I was so angry. Okay, Franny mentioned a wifi café. I grabbed my phone to look it up and saw I had twenty-three missed calls by Ava!

My hands shook as I called back. As it was ringing, a horn blared, causing me to jump back from the curb. I hadn't realized I was beginning to walk across the street.

"What's going on?" I asked when Ava answered before the first ring finished.

"Someone took my mama!"

"Wait, what?"

"She's gone. There's a note. They took her. It's not Valentine's Day yet!" Ava's breath was coming in ragged panicked gasps. "We still had time to get them the money. I don't understand. Jolie, they took my mom!"

"Ava! We'll get her back!" I said sharply, to calm her down. "Are you at the hotel?"

"I'm heading there now."

"Me too, we need to get the money."

Ava and I met at the lobby of the hotel moments later. We rushed up to the room. She punched in the safe's code with a shaking hand. It beeped and didn't open.

"Darn it!" shouted Ava. "Messed it up. Nervous."

"Take a breath. I know it's scary. There is only so much we can do. One thing at a time."

Ava sat back and breathed, then once she was calm, leaned in to enter the code.

She opened the safe as I got the bag and leaned over to grab—the money was gone.

Chapter Eleven

My stomach dropped out, and my brain froze. I felt like I couldn't breathe. When things like this happen to people on TV shows or movies, they always have witty things to say or they are thinking cool things. Me, after an initial brain paralysis, my first thought was we now owed a second loan on the restaurant. How could this be my first thought? Sophia's life was in danger. The Martinez family's business was at stake. Then I looked at Ava. She had managed to crawl to a corner of the room, crumpled up within herself, while I was frozen.

I crawled to her. "Hey, pull it together. What's next? We need a new plan."

She wasn't responding.

I grabbed my phone and video-called Meiser.

"Don't tell me, a third cat?" He grinned at me, then his expression fell. "What's wrong?"

I filled him in then saw Chief Tobias stand up behind Meiser. He must have been at the station.

"Hey, Jolie. Has Ava talked to Delilah at all recently?"

This gave Ava reason to come back to earth.

"Why, what happened to Delilah?"

"Nothing, she's fine. We all got together, since you've been gone, to talk about what we knew was going on with your family. She's willing to help with money if you needed more. Several of us are willing and we've all pulled together to get it ready just in case. She was supposed to contact you to let you know."

Wow. We have some good friends. I love our little village.

Ava must have been beside herself with emotion because her smile, tears, and trembles all came at once as she murmured, "Thank you all so much!"

"Well, Teddy, we all just got the money together yesterday," Meiser reminded. "She may not have had time to call her yet. Lydia was dragging her feet on it before I talked her into it."

Still irked that he *could* talk Lydia into it. Not the right time. Focus, Jolie.

"Ava, you said there was a note. Do you have it?" asked Meiser. She nodded and reached into her pocket and pulled out a crumpled piece of paper. "Okay, you call Delilah now, okay?"

While she did that, I grabbed the note and read it out loud to the guys. It wasn't what I was expecting at all.

This is not how I wanted this to go. Wait for my call.

"There are no directions?" Meiser asked. "Ava, sorry to interrupt. Is this all there was to it?"

She nodded and went back to her conversation with Delilah.

"She said yes. That's all there is to it."

"How did they get the note?" Teddy asked.

"I don't know that yet. She's still talking to Delilah."

"She touched it, and others have too, I take it?" Meiser asked.

"Ugh, yeah," I said, holding it up with my fingers. "I know what you're thinking, but they won't want to get the police involved here. Neither one of us know what's going on or who to trust. There is so much buzz about the Mafia here, and then it's questionable if they're tied in with the police or not."

I noticed Meiser looked uncomfortable when I brought up the Mafia. He had his own demons with family and the Mafia—which, I still planned to look into more when I got back to town. I don't believe in this much coincidence.

"Should I come there?" Meiser asked.

"Definitely not!" I said, maybe a teensy bit too fast. "The fact you all are willing to help us financially is beyond anything we could imagine. We can handle this ourselves on this end."

"And, I will pay you all back," Ava had ended her call with Delilah.

"Oh, you bet you will!" Meiser and Teddy said at the same time with goofy grins on their faces.

Ava rolled her eyes.

"Delilah is coming to you both now," Ava reported to the guys. "She is booking a ticket and coming here with more money. Thanks again and please thank Lydia, Bradley, Betsy, and Keith for me."

Chapter Twelve

Ava had been overwhelmed by everything that had happened after the conversations with the guys and Delilah the night before. We had no way of knowing when we'd get a call or who in the family would get that call. Ava and I had stayed up into the wee hours of the morning going through the I Spy Slides, waiting for a phone call, and discussing what had happened to date.

She told me that her mom was supposed to meet her dad at their house. When she had been two hours late, and after her dad had tried calling, he went out to look for her. When he got to his car, there was the note under the wiper.

Waking up a few hours later, we both had stiff necks from konking out at the table while looking through our PowerPoint and discussing the blackmail. We were still in yesterday's clothes, too.

In mid-stretch, Ava reached for her phone to make sure she hadn't missed any calls. She called her family to ask if they had heard anything and let them know we were on our way there after we showered.

I had grabbed my tote, thinking I threw my phone in there last night, but it wasn't in its normal slot. I began digging around in the mess. I still hadn't organized it since the wreck, and everything was jammed in there. At the bottom of a mound of purse junk, I found the rusty tin can that I had found in the cathedral walls.

"Why do you have trash in your purse?"

"It's not trash. At least, I don't think it is," I said, shaking the can and hearing something bouncing around the aluminum inside.

"What's in it?"

I told Ava about where and how I found it the other day and how I had jammed it in my tote when I got the call from her about the money, then after Lolly and Rafi and everything else—I had forgotten all about it.

"It seems like it's intact. Do we have a can opener?"

"Here, let me see it," Ava said, pulling it out of my hand. "It's got something in it that doesn't sound like it's food."

She shook it and looked at the top, bottom, and sides of the can, then grabbed a pair of scissors and put one blade under the lip of the can and pushed, and it popped open. She turned it upside down and a key and a rolled-up piece of paper slid out.

Ava reached for the key, and I reached for the paper, carefully unrolling it. It was a map, hand-drawn in some sort of ink. I had no clue what the map was of—but in the middle of the map, it had a treasure chest, colored in black ink, with a big black X in the center.

"What on earth?" I asked, holding the map up for Ava to see.

"Is that—" her phone rang, and she sprang for it. "Hello?"

Ava's eyes widened, and she ran to grab paper and pen. "What? No! No! I don't understand." Her voice was shrill with fear. "We still have two more days to get the money to you before anything is supposed to happen."

Ava was bent over shaking, then said, "I want proof of life before I do anything."

Silence. She tried to say confidently, but it came out as a shaky whisper, "No, now." Then she hung up.

"That was them?"

Ava nodded, her eyes red. "They are sending a video of my mom in a few minutes. They'll call either my phone or someone in my family's phone within twenty-four hours with more directions on where to drop the money."

"Is that why you said 'now?'"

"Yes," she burst into tears. "I don't want my mama to have to be with those people another hour.

"Oh honey, come here," I said, reaching for her and hugging her tightly while she cried into my shoulder.

I wish I knew what I could say to help, but I knew there was nothing at this point that could be said or done barring being able to make Sophia magically appear. A thought of Sophia from my childhood popped into my head.

I whispered in Ava's ear, "Let's get gel and toes."

She pulled back with a tear-streaked face and looked at me like I was nuts for a second, then burst into a throaty half-laugh, half-cry.

"I haven't thought of that in forever!"

"It popped into my head." When Ava and I were little, one of Sophia's favorite treats was gelato. Ava and I didn't like the taste of it compared to regular ice cream. Ava always thought it was called 'gel and toes,' and Sophia encouraged her to think that, hoping the disgust of the name would keep us out of her adult treat longer.

"Actually, Mama talks about a place here that has delicious gel and toes." She tapped on her phone. "I guess I should call my family and let them know what I know," she said. Then she froze.

"What?"

"They sent the video."

She hit play. On the screen, we saw a bruised-faced Sophia, in her usual well-put-together outfit and matching jewelry, sitting straight up in a chair. She was tied to the chair and gagged but stared straight into the camera with fire in her eyes: no tears, no fear, but fire and anger. I felt a huge swell of girl-power emotion whoosh through my body.

"Oh, she's fine," I said to Ava.

"She's bruised! They hit her!" Ava cried out.

"She's pissed, Ava. It's time we got pissed, too. Call your family—let's go."

Ava called her dad and filled him in, and then sent the video to him. We got ready to face all of this. On the way to the Martinez home, we stopped to get gelatos and it warmed my heart when Ava asked for gel and toes. The poor kid behind the counter thought she spoke a language he didn't understand—which was partially true.

The only good thing about the twenty-four hours is that Delilah would be here with the money in plenty of time. She was actually already at the Martinez home when we arrived there. Ava ran to her and hugged her, and I saw Ava's body visibly relax simply from having Delilah with her.

"I can't believe everyone pitched in to help us," Ava said to Delilah.

"Huh?"

"With the money. Teddy and Meiser told us how everyone pitched in to help."

Delilah looked away, then down, then fidgeted with her hands before saying, "Right. I know. Everyone loves you both."

"Well, I plan to pay everyone back. I will find a way," Ava said.

"No, you will not, *mija*. This is my debt to you all, and I will take care of it," Thiago said, walking to Delilah and taking her hands in his. "You, my child, are now family. I am sorry it took this for me to realize you complete my daughter."

Ava teared up and put her head on her dad's shoulder.

"Thank you, sir," Delilah said.

"Not 'sir,' please. Maybe Thiago or Papa or Father or Dad."

"Okay—" Delilah took a moment to ponder her choices, "Dad."

I pulled Delilah away while Ava and the family talked.

"You are a horrible liar. It's a good thing Ava is so distracted with this mess, or she would have seen right through you!" I said to Delilah.

"I know. I'm sorry. I can't give her more bad news."

"You mean you don't have the money?" My heart sank.

"No, I have the money."

"Thank God," I exclaimed.

"It's just that I could only get so much together from everyone on such short notice. It wasn't enough. So, I took out a loan from someone."

"From who?"

"Nestle."

"Whaaaat?"

"He's wanted to purchase the buildings, so I sold him a share of one of them to make up the rest of the money we needed. Don't tell Ava. Not now."

"Thiago will pay it back, or we will. It will get fixed first before anyone else. No way are you going to share anything with that man."

I just hoped it wasn't too late.

Delilah, Ava, and I headed to the internet café to go through everything that had happened. We got some blazing hot Earl Grey tea beverages and started from the beginning in a corner booth. Ava couldn't bring herself to unwrap her arms from her girlfriend. She told Delilah everything about Franny and Theo with both arms around her waist and her head on her shoulder. I added what we knew about Rafi and Lolly, all the way up to recently finding the tin can with a key and map in it. Of course, Ava had to disclose all the dirt on me and Kayden—who had seemingly dropped off the face of the earth. I guess I frightened him away, too.

"Wow, Mafia could be involved in all this?" Delilah asked.

"We aren't sure how it all fits together."

"But, we think Franny and Yoselin are somehow tied into it all," Ava said. "The problem is they don't exactly like either one of us."

"Well, they've never seen me before," Delilah said.

"There was a pamphlet there with a number on it," I said, rooting around in my tote, looking for it.

"Oh right, see there have been so many different odd things that have happened. It's difficult to find a pattern between everything," Ava said.

Delilah grinned then grabbed Ava's chin playfully as she said, "My little PI Martinez!"

I laughed, "Yeah, I'm not allowed to use gender-specific pronouns since we aren't sure, and I've been told I don't know how many times to find the pattern."

"Hmm, it looks like a bank account number," Delilah said, grabbing the brochure I pulled out.

"I never thought of that," I said.

"It doesn't look like one from the States. It starts with 'DO,' which I'm assuming stands for 'Dominican.'" Delilah said.

"Wow, she's good," I said.

"She likes to read over my shoulder while I'm studying." Ava smiled. "And, did I tell you this one took shooting lessons?"

"I'll go ask someone," Delilah walked up to the counter to return the empty mugs, looking coyly over her shoulder as I gaped in disbelief.

"Don't you think it's weird that sweet, artsy

Delilah decided to learn to shoot guns?" I asked incredulously.

"We've been in so much hot water the last year, you know it's why I wanted to take these online courses. I think Delilah feels like she needs to protect me."

"Seems extreme, but I'm not a gun person myself," I said.

"So, we could have her try to find some things out, but what? That's what I hate about this," Ava said.

"We've been too personally invested, Ava. We've not been asking the right questions," I said.

Ava looked bewildered as I drifted off into thought.

I had halfway stopped listening, because I was staring at a slide. I flipped through all of them one more time. Things started to fall into place in my head.

Delilah and Ava headed back to the hotel. She was smarter than we had been with the money. She purchased a hard suitcase that locked and kept the money with her everywhere she went, not letting it out of her sight.

I had opted to stay behind to look through things one more time. I decided one more cup of tea couldn't hurt. There was a small line. I recognized one of the women who had slapped Kayden ahead of me in the line. She turned around to see me.

Awkwardly, I waved. "He's not with me today," I said.

"Lucky you," she said.

"You know a different tourist slapped him when we were on a date," I said.

"I'm not a tourist. I grew up here. I've known him and his family forever."

Ava called me before I could ask more.

"What's up?"

"Franny knows where my mom is."

Chapter Thirteen

I wrote down my cell number quickly and gave it to The Slapper, telling her I'd like to talk to her more, but I had to run.

I rushed into our room. Ava was pacing the room with a cell phone on her ear, and Delilah was sitting on the edge of the bed, wringing her hands.

"What's going on?" I asked. "I got here as quick as I could."

"Ava's on the phone with Thiago," said Delilah. "Franny is on her way here now. She has some new information for us about Sophia. Hopefully, she knows where she is."

"Franny's coming *here*?" There was a knock on our door at the same time I said it.

I answered the door with an odd look on my face. She and I weren't too keen on each other. I raised my eyebrows and tightened my lips leading her into the room.

"Papa," Ava announced into the phone. "Franny just got here. I'm putting you on speakerphone."

"He might not want to hear what I have to say," Franny said, fidgeting her fingers nervously.

"Why, what's going on? I demand to know now!" Thiago yelled from the other end of the line. He had been staying at the home front in case there was any contact there.

"Theo came into our restaurant to see me. He said he needed a friend because of something to do with his wife and his brother."

Ava looked ready to tear the curtains to shreds.

"I told him that was not a good idea," Franny said, noting Ava's anger. "He got upset, but as he started to leave, he got a call about Sophia."

"They called *Theo*?" Ava and I said at the same time.

"If he is involved in this, I swear I will kill him," Thiago yelled.

"What did they tell him?" Ava asked.

"I don't know, he took off and wouldn't tell me anything."

"I'm calling Theo now," Thiago said.

Ava started rubbing her face in frustration.

"Ava, show Franny the video of Sophia," I said.

"It can't hurt," she said, grabbing her phone and loading the video.

Franny grabbed a pair of glasses from her purse, slipped them on, and sat to watch the video. She watched it four times, scrutinizing each part of it the last time.

"What?" Ava asked.

"Just give me a minute," she said, starting it over. "Look at this here. Can we blow this up?"

"Here, I can pull it up on my laptop." I pulled the

video up and started fast-forwarding until Franny told me to stop.

"That, right there in the background, on the shelves. Those boxes."

"I know, we tried to zoom in on them, but there are no words," I said.

"The brand on the box. It's hot chocolate," explained Franny. "Everyone around here knows that brand. There's a factory nearby. Come on, let's go check it out. I know the way."

Ava, Delilah, and I looked at each other with fear and hope. Could this be it? Should they trust this woman? There was no time for thought, only action. They all ran outside and piled into Franny's car. Ava dialed Thiago on the drive over, giving him the address.

There were lots of cars in the factory parking lot. Obviously, there were people working a shift. It seemed a strange place to hold someone. I fervently wished we had one of Delilah's guns with us right then.

"There's Dad's car!" Ava pointed as he pulled up. "Figures, this is the Perez family's business," Thiago said and spat on the ground.

"Papa, don't make any assumptions yet."

Delilah, Thiago, Ava, Franny, and I walked inside. Ava strode to the receptionist's desk. "I am the daughter of Thiago Martinez," she said boldly. "I am here to see Mr. Perez."

"He isn't here today," the lady behind the desk said. She made a call for a manager to come to us.

A short, sturdy middle-aged man in a pinstripe suit came through the door. Thiago's body flexed as the man came closer. The two seemed to square off for a moment. Then Thiago visibly lowered his shoulders and exhaled loudly through his nose. They began speaking quietly to one another, then Thiago turned to us and told us to wait there. He and the other gentleman disappeared behind two large doors.

"Do you think that is good news?" I asked, shifting my weight left to right and fidgeting. This all seemed strange.

"I don't know," Ava said.

Six to eight minutes had passed. The receptionist's phone buzzed. "Thiago Martinez has been escorted to the parking lot," she said blandly.

We hustled out, hoping to see Sophia with him somehow, even though Delilah still had the suitcase with her with the money in it.

Instead, Thiago stood dead still, staring at something in his hand. We walked closer, trying to see. It was a human finger, with Caribbean Coral polish on the nail.

Ava had a look that I'd never seen before.

Ava took a breath and looked calm for the first time since all this started. "I want justice," she whispered, "and I don't care how unjustly I get it."

Chapter Fourteen

Thiago found his voice and told them what had transpired.

He had forced one of the Perez brothers to let him go back to the warehouse after showing them the video. The brother swore he knew nothing about it and took Thiago back to the warehouse to help him find the area from the video. When they walked back to the shelving area, there was a finger lying on one of the shelves.

Ava had tried to call the police immediately, but Thiago stopped her. He said if they did anything irrational, it could mean they would lose Sophia forever. Thiago told them that DeShawn, the Perez brother that had led him back to look around the factory, seemed sincerely shocked and angry that his place of business was used to hurt someone and possibly frame the Perezes.

Ava and I were back at the internet café. We'd found that public Wi-Fi in Santo Domingo was spotty at best. This is why the internet café was always hopping, especially tourists who needed their online fix regularly.

"What did you mean before, when you said you started to notice a pattern developing?" asked Ava suddenly. "You also mentioned it was personal."

I pulled up the I Spy Slides. "Look at each slide. There are all kinds of random clues: a brochure with an account number, a hidden tin can with a key and a map—I'll note here too that we've heard a lot about hidden gold around the island from the Mafia, Theo and Franny together. A history of pirates turned mafia who are running around digging holes to bury their gold. All around the place where *your* family has lived for generations *while* being in the bullion business."

"Yeah...?" Ava said, looking perplexed.

"It all ties directly to your family. There's rumors about the Martinez family being involved with the mafia—" Ava started to stand up and leave, but I held my hands up, gave her a stern look to listen, "I'm not saying your family is part of or involved with the mob, Ava. That's my point, why do they need to be when they run the business? Just listen, rumors are going around—but who *said* these things to me—*Kayden* in his tour speech, then we find *his* brochure in La Franny's Bistro. Franny mentioned something about it. It's suspicious, no?"

Before Ava could comment, my phone rang out, and a video call came through from Grandma Opal.

"What's going on?" She demanded with an expression like a bulldog.

"Nothing, Grandma. We're okay. We'll be home soon. How are things there?"

"Hey Mama Opal," Ava said, giving her the peace sign behind me.

"Don't you change the subject on me. Your mother told me about your latest kerfuffle. Are you okay?"

"I'm fine. We're close to being done with things here."

"Everyone here knows about Sophia. How you holdin' up, Ava?"

"I'm doing okay, Mama," Ava had always called my grandma 'mama' but she pronounced it to sound like 'maw-maw' but she also called her mom, 'mama' and pronounced it normally—she was cuckoo like that. "We got a video of Mama. She looked extremely ticked off. It reminded me where I come from," Ava gulped, trying not to tear up.

"That's right, girls. That's why you both have piss and vinegar running through your veins. You're both strong. Survivors. You come from strong women." Grandma held her chin up.

"Whoa, you are wearing make-up, Mama?" Ava asked.

"Yeah, I got my hair done, too. Hold on while I get my selfie stick," she said, putting the phone down on a table, so all we saw was black.

Ava and I gave each other an amused look. I shrugged my shoulders like I don't know what's going on any more than you do.

Grandma came back, putting the phone on a stick.

"Where did you get that, Grandma?"

"Mick got it for me," she said, positioning the phone. We got a good look at some cleavage for a moment—a little too much cleavage on a grandma if you ask me.

"What? Why on earth is Mick buying you a

selfie-stick?" I asked.

"I told him I want to be able to get my body involved in my selfies. He suggested a selfie stick. So, he ordered me one. Now look, I want you to see my outfit for my date." She held the phone up in M&M's, where she was standing by a table. I could see onlookers grinning.

Grandma had a low-cut royal blue blouse on with the buttons unbuttoned three down. She had on black slacks and cute little flats. Her hair was very fluffy and full, and she had on bright red lipstick and her nails were done, too.

"Who's the lucky guy?" Ava asked, elbowing me in the side and grinning.

"Thomas Costello. He's taking me to an early-bird dinner. Mick has new special prices between three and six every day of the week now. I talked him into it."

Wow, Meiser and my family seemed to be closer than he and I were.

"Nice," Ava said.

Just then, Tom, or Thomas, as my grandma called him, came up to the table and said, "Hey, sexy lady," and handed her a huge bouquet of red roses.

Grandma must have forgotten that we were there because she set the phone on the table with the camera up. We could see Tom, in a fancy suit, leaning over to kiss grandma on the cheek. She turned her face and nailed him on the lips. His eyes bulged out. He pulled back momentarily and smiled at her and said, "Let's save this for the bedroom."

Grandma reached for his collar and pulled him into her, planting a wet kiss on his mouth.

I threw my phone at Ava, screaming, "Make it stop!!! Make it stop now!! Please turn it off!"

Ava looked at the screen, and her eyebrows shot up. "Go get yours, girl!" she yelled into the phone, then fell over in her chair, laughing. It was good to see her laugh again for a moment. But then she frowned, like she caught herself being happy and felt bad. I rubbed her arm.

"No, listen, Ava," I persisted. "What I was trying to say before the phone call was ... the common factor here isn't your family. It's--"

She glanced up and her eyes widened, then she pointed at the door.

Kayden had just walked into the café, holding Yoselin's hand.

Chapter Fifteen

I shoved Ava's finger down, so they didn't notice us.

Speak of the devil!

I grabbed Ava and pushed her toward the back of the room, ducking into the crowd.

"What are you doing? Stop pushing me!"

"I forgot to tell you something weird happened yesterday here. One of those women that slapped Kayden was in here. I assumed she was a tourist. She said she's known him forever."

We watched Kayden and Yoselin grab coffee and sit down at one of the public computers. It was weird, because it looked like Kayden had make-up on for some odd reason.

"You just said something about him and Franny. You are confusing me. Do you mean they are all in this blackmail thing or are they all *romantically* involved?"

"I don't know. I'm trying to figure it out. Maybe all three of them are doing both?"

"*You* were involved with him," Ava said.

"For a hot minute," I said.

"Yeah, it was hot, wasn't it?" Ava's phone rang and she put it to her ear, sticking her finger in her other ear so she could hear over the noise of the crowd.

"Hello?"

She had that same look from the other night. I knew it was "the call." I looked over and noticed that Yoselin had stepped away from Kayden and was on her phone.

Ava got off the phone and began dialing.

"What's going on?"

"It's time to bring the money. I'm calling Delilah," Ava said.

"Put her on speaker—come here in the restroom so we can hear better," I said, knocking to make sure no one was in there.

Ava followed me in, continuing to talk to her girlfriend on speakerphone. "Delilah, I just got the call. I'm supposed to go to this rental car place and ask for a specific type of car, then I have directions on where to go and what time with the money. Can you meet me at the rental car business with the money?"

"Where and what time is the meeting?" I asked.

"I'm not telling either of you. This is my family, and I will handle it from here."

"NO WAY!" Delilah and I sang out at the same time.

"Yes, that was their instructions to me. Come alone, or my mama dies. I'm not risking that, and I'm not risking either of you getting hurt."

"Ava, be smart here. You are better off with us coming with you. They don't need to know," I said.

"I have an idea. We'll trick them," Delilah said. Ava, you go and get the car. If they are telling you where and what type of car to get, then let me go in a black hoodie, get the car, and you put a black hoodie on too, then I'll meet you somewhere and get in the trunk so they don't know I'm there," Delilah said.

"Perfect," I said. "I'd feel so much better about that. If you agree to go with Delilah, then I will follow Yoselin."

"Why?" Ava asked.

"Because she was on the phone the same time you were," I said.

"Delilah, are you sure about this?" Ava asked.

"Baby, you know I'm all in with you!"

I grinned at Ava and nodded in agreement.

"Okay," Ava said. "Wish us luck."

She headed out of the bathroom. I stayed for a moment to get myself together. I called an Uber to have them meet me there. Hopefully, I could get a person who was willing to follow someone. I looked to make sure I had plenty of money.

I went back out front, but both Kayden and Yoselin were gone. Crap on a stick!

I saw someone heading toward the public computer where they had been sitting. I lurched forward and jammed my behind in the seat. Looking up, I saw an annoyed young man. "Oh, sorry, I had been here with a friend and didn't realize he left so I wanted to get the same computer."

He rolled his eyes and moved on.

Okay, I am not tech-savvy at all. I had no clue

where to begin. I called Bradley, Leavensport's local journalist, all-around writer, and also, tech wizard.

"Hey girl, how's it going?"

"Good, Bradley. I'm in a rush, sorry—I'm at a public computer and want to know what the people that were here before us were looking at. Do you know how I can find that or is there no way?"

"If they were lazy about clearing their browsing history and logging out of their email before they left, it should be easy."

"They left in a hurry, so I may have gotten lucky."

Bradley continued to explain step-by-step things to do to find out what people had looked into. I gingerly clicked backward through the browsing history until I hit an email account: bluebeard78@gmail.com.

Still logged in. "HECK YES!" I shrieked in the middle of the café. On the phone, Bradley bemoaned the fate of his eardrum as the café patrons glared at me. I began clicking through the emails.

"That's it. I think I have what I need," I said, seeing an interesting email attachment.

"Good, is Ava doing okay with everything?" he asked. It seemed like he was still struggling with his old feelings for Ava and the idea that she and his sister were in a relationship now.

It was an awkward situation.

"She's doing as well as can be expected. Delilah has been great. How are you and Lydia doing?"

"We're not. We're over. She's pregnant," he said.

"What?!? Pregnant? Are you sure? Is it yours? Why would you break up?" I was being a bit nosey, but this was big news.

Then I had a thought. Oh, good Lord! Maybe Lydia and Meiser were a thing.

"I'm sorry to hear that." I heard a beep. "Hey Bradley, again, sorry, I have to go, I have another call coming in." I wish I had time to digest all this.

"Sure thing—take care."

I answered, hoping it was Ava or Delilah, "Hello?"

"It's Sandra," a voice said.

"Who?"

"The woman you gave your number to at the café yesterday. The one who slapped Kayden."

"Oh yeah, thanks for getting back with me."

"What is your friend's last name?" she asked.

"Martinez."

"Ah, no wonder Kayden was so interested in you both. He always has a reason."

"Why?" I asked while opening the email and seeing an audio recording as an attachment at the same time.

"Because he is a Perez. *Perez Rich and Creamy Hot Cocoa.* I can't believe he didn't pull the whole hot chocolate thing with you. That's his go-to for women—chocolate. We've all fallen for it. It's delicious."

"Wait? That isn't his last name. It's Kayden Rodriguez." I said, getting ready to click on the recording.

She laughed. "More games. No, he is most definitely a Perez."

I listened to the recording, then grabbed my tote and took off, hoping the Uber was still waiting for me.

I headed out the door, looking around, and saw a vehicle with a person waving a hand out the window at me. I ran to get in. The person got out to open the door for me.

"Oh no, I'm in a rush—"

Blackness.

Chapter Sixteen

I felt like I had been zapped with a thousand volts. My body ached. I couldn't wake up. I heard a voice.

"Jolie, wake up. Wake up, my beautiful girl."

I opened my eyes. It was Mick. He was looking me over, rubbing my forehead and pushing my hair back. I smiled at him.

"Why do I hurt?" I asked.

"I think they Tased you."

That statement startled me enough to move around, but I yelled out in pain. Where was I? It was a small cot or cell of some kind with one toilet and one old torn, dirty mattress on the cement floor.

I looked again and realized it wasn't Meiser, but Sophia who was comforting me. I must have been dreaming.

"What? Are you okay?" I grabbed her hands, looking over all her digits and counting to ten.

"Child, did they drug you or something?" Sophia asked, pulling her hands back.

"No, Thiago found a severed finger at the hot chocolate factory that had fingernail polish on it that is the same coral color that you were wearing. It scared us all to death!"

"Oh, no! Not *my* finger."

"What's going on?"

"Family wars is my best guess."

"Sophia, how angry would you be if I asked if the Martinez family has ever been a part of the mob?"

"You've heard some of the rumor mill in our area?"

"Not from anyone I'd consider reputable. But I'm only asking because it's come up, and all this is happening."

"What Ava told you is true. Thiago's family has been in the gold business for generations. The Martinez name is known for it. That became dangerous back in the day with pirates. And I'm talking way back in the day when Francis Drake and the English stormed the island."

"Yikes, it goes way back."

"Yes, it does. Thiago takes a lot of pride in his family and what they've worked for and a big reason for that pride is they have done so without criminal activity. Now, don't get me wrong, my dear, the family got into some trouble here and there. In the past, they've battled other families in trying to keep a monopoly on the gold business. And I won't say that I agree with that, but there you have it. My Thiago has never been that kind of man, though. He would not think of fighting for a monopoly. He didn't think something like that was worth the discord."

"So, is that where the Martinez/Perez family

feud came from?"

"Yep, that's it, alright. Before Thiago's time, there was a lot of feuding. The Perez family was supposedly pirates who eventually got into the mob business. They stole the Martinez gold and, according to folklore, they've buried it all around the island."

"And is Kayden the one who kidnapped you and blackmailed your family?" I couldn't hide the venom in my voice. I had let that man touch me.

"Kayden Perez? I doubt it. He's not like the rest of his family."

I was surprised to hear Sophia defend him.

"Kayden is involved with his family. But he's immune to all the mob activity because of what he's been through recently."

"I don't understand. When Ava and I were with him, two different women came up and slapped him across the face at two different times. I thought they were tourists but ran into one of them who said she grew up with him, and she made it seem like he was a scoundrel."

"Oh, Kayden has always loved the ladies. But he found his true love, got married, and they had a beautiful daughter, Tatiana."

"He's married?" My jaw hit the floor.

"She died in childbirth. Tatiana is six. That's why his father has allowed Kayden to do his own thing. They want to protect the little one. They have some scruples, at least."

"Oh my gosh. He never said a word. So, who took you?"

"I don't know. I've barely had any contact. All I know is, it's a man. But no, to answer your original question, our family has never been involved with the Mafia. We were pressured to join before the girls were born. That's why Thiago moved us to Ohio."

"Right, Ava said his friend bought shares or something and took over to try and keep the business afloat while avoiding having to get involved with the mob, right?"

"Ron Rene. They were best friends. He passed, though. Theo and Rafi are his sons."

"Why did Rafi come back to take over and not Theo?"

"Because of our Lolly. They both fell for her in—"

The door opened, and a man in a mask came in and pointed a gun at us.

"Let's go, ladies," the voice was distorted. I could see a lump in the throat under the mask—some voice modulator.

"Where are we?" I asked, walking out. It was damp and dark. Were we inside a cave? That made sense; there were no windows in the cell. I doubted that the toilet was attached to any plumbing.

"You should know, I told you this is the place you should visit first," said the strange robotic voice. "You never took my advice."

"So, I know you?" It was weird. This was like a combination of a cave and a warehouse. I had no idea what the person meant by they told me to come here.

"Jolie, don't ask. We don't want to see his face," Sophia said, grabbing my arm.

"She's smart," the person said, removing the voice box and pulling the mask off. "If you see my face, it means there is no way I'm letting you get out of here alive. See, I told you to visit Three-Eyes Park."

Rafi. Sophia and I stood, frozen in complete shock.

"What are you doing? After all we've done for you?" Sophia spat out.

Rafi laughed out loud. "Your family has done nothing but cause me grief. You are all the reason why my father is dead."

"We would have never done anything to Ron Rene," Sophia cried. "Thiago loved him like a brother."

"Okay, that's why he left us here to deal with everything while your family ran to the States?" Rafi growled.

"Your father had a way out. That's what he told Thiago. But I was pregnant. They were threatening us. Please stop this, Rafi. Don't involve my Ava or others in this."

"Wait. I don't understand. You never told me about any places to visit in Santo Domingo," I said, thinking back to what he said a couple of minutes ago.

"Sure, I did—when we first met. But, I also had my partner whisper it in your ear. I've heard from Theo and Lolly how nosey you and Ava are. I figured given enough time around the island, one of you would find something of use. And, you didn't let me down. Not only did you get me fifty grand, but now I've got another fifty on the way. I sent Ava a video of you passed out in the trunk of the car."

"Whose finger did Thiago find?" Sophia asked.

"A nobody. A homeless woman that was passed out drunk," Rafi said nonchalantly.

Sophia and I gasped in horror.

"Oh, she was so drunk she didn't feel a thing. I'm the one who had to clean the finger up, find a good nail to glue on, and then get the right color so you thought it was Sophia's finger," Rafi seemed very proud of himself.

At that point, there was a knock on the door. Rafi looked at a camera on his phone and said, "Pull the hood down so I can see your face."

She must have done it because Rafi buzzed her in.

Ava kept her head down, walking toward Rafi. I didn't even think she knew who had kidnapped us. It was odd that she was keeping her head looking straight down at her feet, not looking at any of us. Rafi seemed confused as well.

Rafi had his gun on Ava as she moved toward him. "Walk the money up to me, Ava."

Ava stopped a few feet in front of him.

The door swung open, and Delilah came running in, shooting a gun wildly. Stunned from my confusion of Ava's odd head-behavior, I grabbed Sophia and hit the ground.

"*Ten Cuidado, mija!*" Sophia yelled to Ava.

Rafi fired a shot. Sophia twisted away from my protective grasp, staggering to her feet in an animal rage. She leaped on his back, beating him with her fists. He grunted in surprise and pain and tried to shove her away, but she punched him hard in the side of the head and he staggered, throwing both of them off balance. Sophia lost her grip and stumbled backward. The moment that Sophia was clear, Delilah fired once at Rafi, and he fell to the ground.

"Mama," Ava screamed, running to her.

I ran behind Ava and grabbed Rafi's gun.

"I'm fine, *mija,* I'm not hit," Sophia said. "Are you okay?"

"I'm fine, Mama!" Then Ava turned on Delilah. "You didn't tell me you had a gun!"

"It's a good thing I did, too! It's over now. We're all safe."

"You look weird with your head down and your hair falling in your face," I said to Ava.

"Yeah, it was meant to cause uncertainty."

"Well, it definitely worked," Sophia said putting her arm around Ava's shoulder.

I called the police, and we waited in tense silence.

Chapter Seventeen

We had fearfully waited for the police last night after the terror of the gunshots. I think Delilah needs to keep taking those lessons. The fear was wondering if the police were in on it or not. They did take Rafi in, and later, we learned that Kayden and Yoselin were a part of the entire scheme, too. We were all gathered around the dinner table at the Martinez home the next night where Sophia was finally safe and sound.

"So, Rafi got involved with the Mafia when he came back from Ohio to take over for his father?" I asked.

"Seems so. Rafi had a gambling problem that no one knew about. He used the Mafia to cover bets, and that got our business tied up with them. He knew his father's wishes and that I wanted nothing to do with the mob. So, they used that against him."

Theo was absent from the dinner table. Lolly had filed for separation. As far as we all knew, he had no idea about his brother's criminal doings, but Lolly was less than happy to hear about Theo sniffing around Franny again.

"Wait, this is nuts. So, Rafi kidnapped Tatiana and used that to blackmail Kayden to do his dirty work for him?"

"It is mind-boggling to me that the Sanchez boys have grown into cheaters, gamblers, kidnappers, blackmailers, and mobsters. Their father will turn over in his grave," Thiago said.

"Rafi was at the root of all of this because he owed money to the mob. He took Tatiana to get Kayden to do some things for him. How do Yoselin and Franny play into it all?" I asked.

"They grew up in poverty," Lolly explained. "Rafi knew them. He fronted them mob money to open their business, but then started demanding ridiculous interest because of his own debts. He started strong-arming them." She shook her head in disgust. "He's the one who attacked Franny and took the deposit money from her. And he threatened Franny into seducing Theo." Her lip curled. "Rafi supposedly was in love with me in Ohio, and then when we all moved back, he had some sort of weird obsession with me. Franny tried to say no, but that's when he started the fire while Franny and Yoselin were in their restaurant. It was a huge story here, and they named it The Valentine's Day fire. That frightened them enough to do what he wanted."

"Wow, this is Shakespearean," I said, putting my hands on the table and shaking my head slowly back and forth. I had even seen the article about the fire that started on February fourteenth, but I didn't read the Hollywood-type name they gave it or maybe I could have put that together with the date. I was still a tad confused by it all. But it all seemed to boil down to family feuds and drama. "So, Franny and Yoselin knew that Rafi was the one who beat up Franny and took the deposit money?"

"Yeah, the girls wanted out," explained Lolly. "They liked you two. I guess Franny could not give a care about me, though. But yeah, Rafi found out I had threatened her earlier. He was already upset with them, and then I had denied his advances for Lord knows how many times, so he thought he'd get payback."

"But he paid your bail," I said, confused.

"Playing the hero and probably to take suspicion off himself is my best guess," Lolly said. "Also, he originally wanted the money on Valentine's Day because he planned to take it, then kidnap me. But Yoselin took the money from your safe too soon, setting everything into motion."

"Wait, so Yoselin stole the money from the safe in our hotel?" Ava asked.

That was a good point. Somehow in all the drama, I had forgotten about that.

"Yes, it was Yoselin. I guess she got temporary work as a waitress in the bar to get access to the rooms."

So, it was Yoselin I saw that night in the bar! I thought she looked familiar. "How'd she get access to the safe? I can see stealing a room key, but the safe combo?"

"Again, I'm assuming she manipulated and conned her way into a relationship with the right person. Or, who knows, it was Rafi who wanted that money so he could get more. He could have used someone to strong-arm management into giving her the combo."

"WOW! And the plot thickens," I said, shaking

my head, then added, "How is Tatiana?"

"She's with the Perez family. Rafi's future isn't looking too bright, and not because he's in jail. Those men would do anything for that girl. Kayden is currently in jail for his part, but the Perez family has a lot of pull. They'll get him out on bond. Kayden is the one that attacked you based on Rafi's orders."

That's why it looked like he had make-up on—he had a scratch on his face that I gave him. Boy I really know how to pick men!

"What about Yoselin?" Ava asked.

"She's not so fortunate. Hopefully, she can obtain a good enough lawyer to get her a deal to plea down. Those girls are in a financial hole right now with everything that has happened and their families do not have a lot of money," Sophia said.

"I feel bad for them," Lolly said.

"I can't believe you'd say that after everything Franny put you through," Thiago said.

"Don't get me wrong. I don't want to be best friends with her, but Rafi put her up to it. He forced her into it. When she had a choice this last time, she told Theo no. Then, she helped find Mama."

"That is true, Thiago. We are getting much of our money back that Rafi used. Not all, but we will be fine. Maybe we should help those girls out." Sophia reached for her husband's hand.

"I'll pay our lawyer to handle Yoselin's case, and I'll look into what they owe for their restaurant." He smiled at his wife.

I was sucking down the rest of my bubble tea and eyeballing the jerk chicken, beans, and rice for seconds. Carmen was an amazing cook. I loved that she was eating with us and getting to enjoy her food. I had her sit next to me so I could take notes on this jerk sauce for the chicken.

Scooping some more stew, I asked, "So the account number on the pamphlet that I found, the tin can with the key and map. What was that all about?"

Carmen had gotten up to refill my bubble tea, which I was grateful for because the jerk chicken was delicious but spicy.

"My understanding is that Kayden wrote the account number down for Yoselin. She was to take the money from the safe in your hotel room and put it in Rafi's account. That was part one of the plan for Rafi to get a portion of money he owed to the Valendro mob. I think Rafi knew he was going to get caught eventually. He was trying to get out of my business since I was back and get into the cement business with the Valendros. They are another rival family to the Perez family. Actually, it's thanks to the Valendros that we could come back. They got into the game of cement and gold and began working with the mob. Unfortunately, Rafi's gambling addiction got him in trouble and mixed up with it all," Thiago said.

"And his Lolly addiction," Ava grinned.

"Shut up!" Lolly hit Ava on the arm.

"And the map?" I asked again.

"Turns out it may not be folklore that all those years ago there is Martinez gold buried around the island," Sophia said. "Supposedly, one of the women back then saw the men burying it and drew a map. It is said, after sleeping with the pirate, she waited until he slept, stole the key to the treasure chest where she saw him put the gold, and put the key and the map in a tin can. She went to reflect at the cathedral walls, and when the pirate came looking for her, she found a rock to put it behind. She shared it with her daughter who shared it with her daughter and so on. Who knows, there could be buried treasure somewhere. Rafi would love to have gotten his hands on that."

"Wait, so why wouldn't they go and take the gold then?" I asked.

"The story goes that the pirate found out she hid the map and key and killed her. But he was killed in a battle within days. This story has been passed down from generation to generation. People have looked for the can. I am guessing someone at some point had to have found it because it was changed to a fake rock that is more modern. Why they never went for the gold? Who knows? The map is so old– maybe it doesn't make sense where it is? Or maybe someone found it for all we know."

Ava, Delilah, and I decided to spend a few more nights with the Martinezes' to relax before heading back to Leavensport. Also, I had to check on Meiser's new cat, pay, and make sure I knew all the ins and outs for getting him on the plane and to the States.

Chapter Eighteen

February 20, 2020

Well, there is no "new" man like I had hoped for. It turns out, he was not someone to be trusted either. My first reaction was to put walls up. Although this trip has been filled with romance, blackmail, kidnappings, and mob activity, it's also been an opportunity for me to walk away from my family and my life in Leavensport and really think about where I am and what I want for my future.

I've watched Ava grow in her relationship with Delilah over time to the point where she's ready to ask her to marry her. I watched Delilah drop everything for Ava and put a lot at risk for her, too. While here, I tried to be the carefree girl to have a one-night stand, but that's definitely not who I am. I realized that Meiser is ingrained in my life at this point, whether I want him to be or not. He's just there. And that makes me happy. But now, there's this news about Lydia and I don't know what to think or feel.

That brings me back into the vicious cycle—and

that's not where I want to be. I do know that. Meiser and I agreed to talk and be completely honest. So, I'll find out where he stands with everything. In the meantime, it's time for me to pursue a life where I'm avoiding stepping on cracks all the time.

Coming home will be good for me. This seems so minute, but one thing I'm so proud of is while here, I kept my family at bay when I needed space. Ignoring calls at times and standing up to my mom. More than that, after standing up to her, Meiser tried to make me feel guilty for going too hard on her, and I didn't allow myself to feel guilty AND I stood up to him, too.

So, a big goal for me moving forward is "adulting" with boundaries intact with family and also accepting who I am without guilt. I'm over believing I don't need therapy or to figure things out. Obviously, I needed it, and I need to continue to grow and learn tools to take care of myself.

Some next steps for me will be figuring things out with Chuck, once and for all. Also, I need to sit down with my family, and we all need to hash all this family drama out. Everyone else in the family will have to figure out for themselves what they want to hold onto as far as anger and regrets go. That's their issues to deal with—me, I want to get to know my Aunt and Uncle and cousins moving forward—as long as they want the same.

Lastly, I believe I'm ready to be in a relationship with the right person and move forward. Who that is, I've yet to find out.

I'm looking forward to our next session.

Thank you for your patience with me as I work through things.

Sincerely,
Jolie Tucker

Chapter Nineteen

"How was the flight back?" Grandma Opal asked, holding hands with Tom, who was staring at her lovingly.

"We made it in one piece. Although we were almost banned from the airline before we even boarded, thanks to Ava," I said.

"You know I was right!" Ava exclaimed.

"Do tell," my mom said.

My family, Meiser, and our Leavensport gang that we grew up with were all gathered at Cast Iron Creations after hours. I had made a huge Dominican meal for everyone that included Sancocho, red beans, and rice, and jerk chicken. Ava had figured out how to master the bubble tea, and we were definitely putting that stuff on the menu! It was a tad awkward having Lydia there, knowing she was pregnant. No one would notice to look at her, but I knew. I wasn't aware of who knew and who didn't so I kept my big mouth shut for now. Bradley was sitting at the opposite end of the table from her. I noticed she was sitting by Mick though. I also noticed that he was, in fact, using a cane regularly since we got back.

"Well, as you all know, we brought Lucky, the orange cat, home with us and he is now an official member of the Meiser family," I said, holding a hand out for display toward Meiser who grinned at me and took a bow.

I continued, "Ava tried to get frequent flier miles for the cat. She argued the point and almost wore the poor lady at the ticket counter out, but people began complaining so much in line that a manager came out."

"He was a weasel himself," Ava said.

"You didn't have to tell him that if weasels like him could get frequent flier miles that the cat should be able to, too," I said.

Everyone at the table cracked up.

"Well, it's the truth!" Ava said.

My cousin Tink was sitting next to me. "You know, there really is a thing where some airlines will include pets with those mile rewards."

"See! I knew I was right!" Ava declared.

"Tink, don't get her started," I said, smiling at him. My cats were so spoiled after a stay-ca with their new favorite person. Tink liked to eat ham sandwiches and now my cats all expected a ham fix daily.

"I'm not kidding, they really do," he said, cackling.

"In all seriousness," Ava began, "I want to take a quick minute to thank every one of you. All of you banded together to help my family and me at a horrible time. I'm so grateful for everything you all did. So, I'm not great at saying thanks, but thanks."

Her eyes welled up.

"Geesh, it's like you won an academy award or something," Meiser teased her to lighten up the mood.

I rolled my eyes, then got up to clear some of the plates. Delilah helped me. We were in the kitchen alone when I said, "So, we all have our money back. You paid Nestle back, right?"

She stopped scrubbing a pan and looked at me.

"I don't like that look," I said.

"It's complicated."

Uh-oh.

Chapter Twenty

The next day I finally was sitting in Tabitha's office discussing the last few weeks' events and the content of my letters to her, journals, and some voice memo recordings I had been trying.

"The guilt is still something I struggle the most with in all of this," I said. "For example, when I saw that the money was stolen out of the safe at the hotel, my first thought was that it was a second mortgage. NOT Sophia's safety. What does that say about me?"

"That you're human. It doesn't mean you are a horrible person because you have an initial thought in a state of panic. You said yourself your next feeling was guilt in not thinking of Sophia first. You were under a lot of pressure and stress. Also, it says a lot about you that you dropped everything to go be with Ava and help her and her family. That's loyalty."

"I know. Guilt is something I always have a hard time with."

"Every caring, loving person does. Guilt isn't a

bad thing or the enemy, Jolie. Allowing it to control your life is a bad thing. Feeling it from time to time means you are a caring, loving, and giving person. Just don't let it consume you and drive you in your life. The trick for all of us is finding balance, stepping back when we need to and reflecting, and regrouping to move forward. It's always a struggle."

"That's where my perfectionist ways kick in. I think I should be able to do that on auto-pilot, and if I can't, then there's something wrong with me."

"Yes, but you didn't realize or understand that before. You figured that and a lot out on your own. This trip was stressful and not the best of ways to get out of town. But it was good for you. I'm happy with your progress and how much you've learned on your own. We can really begin to dig in and start to deal with a lot of things moving forward."

"That's the plan," I said.

"What's the biggest thing you think you learned?" Tabitha watched me with her head tipped to one side, tapping her pen on her lower lip.

"I've shared with you about my bio father's suicide attempt and how, when I was taken away from him, he wailed like an animal being hurt." I looked off into space as I spoke. "I realized whenever someone, especially a man, lets me down, I feel that same way as that moment. I panic for fear of not being wanted and them leaving, and I put up walls. I learned that walls don't protect me—they keep me hidden. I'm setting a goal for myself to be able to be capable of assessing each individual situation and protecting myself. I can take care of myself."

"That's a wonderful lesson." Tabitha smiled broadly. "As you said in your letter to me, you are learning the difference between walls and boundaries. And there is a huge difference."

I left the office feeling refreshed. Getting into my car, I looked across the road and saw Meiser's car. He got out using his cane and limped over to open the passenger door to help a second person out.

Lydia.

He rubbed her belly, and they walked into the OBGYN's office together.

Recipes
Blueberry Cobbler
(*This recipe came from
www.thecookingchanneltv.com)

Ingredients
- 1/2 cup unsalted butter
- 1 cup all-purpose flour
- 1 1/2 teaspoons baking powder
- 1 teaspoon minced dried lavender
- 1/2 teaspoon salt
- 1 cup whole milk
- 1 cup granulated sugar plus 1 tablespoon
- Juice and zest of 1 lemon
- 1 scraped vanilla bean
- 2 cups blueberries
- Vanilla bean ice cream or lightly sweetened whipped cream, for serving, optional

Directions
Preheat the oven to 350 degrees F. Place the butter in a 10-inch cast-iron skillet and transfer to the preheated oven to melt.

Meanwhile, mix together the flour, baking powder, lavender and salt in a bowl. Stir in the milk, 1 cup sugar, the lemon juice, zest and vanilla to combine. Mix together the remaining tablespoon sugar and the blueberries in another bowl. Remove the hot skillet with the melted butter from the oven and pour in the batter. Top with the sugared blueberries. Bake until brown and the batter has risen up and around the fruit, about 30 minutes.

Transfer to a rack to cool slightly. Serve with vanilla bean ice cream or lightly sweetened whipped cream.

Sancocho Dominican Style Soup

(*This recipe comes from
https://www.mrsislandbreeze.com/recipe-
items/sancocho-dominican-style-soup/)

*Be sure to use a Dutch Cast Iron Pan to pull out all
of the flavors in this delicious Caribbean soup!

Ingredients

- 1lb of beef, cubed for stewing
- 1 1/2lb of chicken drumettes
- 1 smoked ham hock
- 1 lime
- 2 cloves of garlic
- 1 teaspoon of oregano
- 1 teaspoons of paprika
- 4 tablespoons of salt
- 1/4 cup of parsley
- 1 tablespoon of adobo
- 2 firm, yellow plantains
- 2 white yams
- 1 chayote
- 1 white sweet potato
- 1/2 small pumpkin
- 15 chili piquins
- 2-3 tablespoons of vegetable or canola oil
- 1 cup of chicken broth
- 6 cups of water

Directions

1. Place the beef into a large mixing bowl.
2. Cut the lime in half and squeeze the juice of

half of the lime over the beef.

3. Peel and mince the garlic cloves and add them into the bowl with the beef.

4. Chop a 1/4 cup of fresh parsley and add it into the bowl with the beef as well and stir.

5. Cover the bowl with saran wrap or foil and place it in the refrigerator for at least 30 minutes.

6. Empty the chicken into a separate bowl and squeeze the remaining half of lime over the chicken.

7. Sprinkle the adobo, paprika, and two tablespoons of salt over the chicken, stir, and then set the chicken aside.

8. Peel the sweet potato, yams, chayote, and plantain, cut them into medium sized chunks, and set them aside.

9. Cut the pumpkin in half, clean out the seeds, remove the skin, and cut the pumpkin into medium sized chunks.

10. In a large cast iron pot, bring the oil to a medium-high heat.

11. Remove the beef from the refrigerator and put the beef in the cast iron pot.

12. Brown the beef for 2-3 minutes, then turn the stove down to a medium heat, cover the cast iron pot and allow the beef to cook for 12-13 more minutes. Add a few tablespoons of broth or water if necessary to make sure that the beef does not burn.

13. After 15 minutes has passed, add the chicken drumettes into the cast iron pan. Stir the chicken and beef together, then cover the cast iron pan and allow the chicken to cook for 5-6 minutes.

14. Add the water, smoked ham hock and chicken broth to the pot and bring the soup

to a boil.

15. Turn the stove down to a medium heat and add the yams, sweet potato, and chayote. Stir the soup, cover it, and allow it to cook for 15 minutes. (Tip: Be sure to stir the soup occassionally and leave the pot cover slightly lifted so that the soup does not bubble out of the pot and onto the stove.)

16. After 15 minutes have passed, add the pumpkin and plantain to the soup. Stir the soup a few times, cover the pot, and allow the soup to cook for 10 minutes.

17. Add in the chili piquins and allow the soup to cook for 2-3 more minutes.

Optional: Add in one tablespoon of salt.

Grab your ladle and bowls, serve, and enjoy.

Servings : 9-10

Ready in : 95 Minutes

La Bandera "The Flag"

(*This recipe comes from
https://theturquoisetable.com/la-bandera-a-
traditional-dish-from-the-dominican-republic/)

First, the Dominican sofrito rub for storing and
cooking meat

Ingredients

- 1 green bell pepper, seeded and chopped
- 1 green bell pepper, seeded and chopped
- 1 red bell pepper, seeded and chopped
- 1 Italian pepper, seeded and chopped
- 1 bunch of cilantro leaves, chopped
- 1 bunch of culantro leaves, chopped
- 9-10 cloves of garlic, whole
- 1 large red or spanish onion chopped
- 1 bunch of scallions, chopped
- 2 plum tomatoes, cut into slices or chunks
- 1 Tablespoon dried oregano
- 1/4 cup white distilled vinegar
- 1 chicken bullion cube
- 6-8 Sweet peppers also known as ajices dulces

Directions

Add all ingredients, a bunch at a time to a food
processor and process until smooth. Transfer to a
large mason jar with a tight fitting lid and place in
the refrigerator until ready to use. Alternatively,
you can portion the sofrito in ice cube trays and
freeze. Once frozen transfer the sofrito cubes into
Ziploc bags and store.

Notes

Ajices dulces: The color of these peppers range
from a light to medium green, yellow, red and
orange. They pack some heat - Therefore, you may
want to reduce the amount to 1-2 or omit
completely.

In case you're having trouble identifying
cilantro, cilantro is identified by its long leaves and
serrated edges.

Next, the La Bandara!

Ingredients
- dry oregano
- pepper
- adobo seasoning
- Worcestershire sauce
- 2 cloves of garlic
- 1/2 red onion
- handful of parsley
- 1lb beef top round steak

Directions

Wash the beef and place it in a large bowl. Add
the chopped garlic. onions and parsley. Add about a
teaspoon of ground pepper. Season with a few
sprinkles of adobo powder... about 1/2 tablespoon.
Add 2 tablespoons of Worcestershire sauce and mix
well. Cover and place in refrigerator for at least 2
hours. Heat up a skillet on med-high heat and add
the steaks. Turn them so they cook on both sides
and cover them. After 10 minutes the meat should
be mostly cooked. Remove the steaks and place
them on a plate.

Lastly, the Dominican Beans—believe me, it is worth the prep and time for this meal!

Ingredients
- 1 tsp of canola or vegetable oil
- 1 cup of chicken stock
- 1 large can of red beans
- 2 tablespoons of tomato paste
- adobo seasoning powder
- dry oregano
- 1 stalk of celery
- 1/4 red onion
- 2 garlic cloves
- apple cider vinegar
- parsley

Directions
1. Chop up the onion and celery in chunks. Peel the garlic but leave whole and tie up the parsley into a knot. Heat up the oil and add the onions, garlic and celery until the onion starts getting brown.
2. Add the beans and the parsley. Next, add 1/2 tbs of dry oregano and about 1/2 tbs of adobo. Mix that well and add the tomato paste. Add one cup of chicken stock. If you are vegetarian add vegetable stock or water. If adding water just make sure to add a little bit more adobo to taste.
3. Mix well until the tomato paste is mostly dissolved. Cook covered on medium-low heat.
4. Once they are boiling add a splash of vinegar.

Mix the vinegar in and lower the heat once they start boiling so they don't burn.

5. Add a tablespoon of tomato paste to the skillet where the steaks were cooking (do not throw away the juices the steak gave out).

6. Add a cup of water or chicken stock and dissolve the tomato paste as much as you can.

7. Add the steaks to the skillet and cover. Cook on low heat for 10 minutes.

Homemade Bubble Tea

(* I took this recipe from
https://healthynibblesandbits.com/how-to-make-
bubble-tea/ --what's great about this site is that she
goes into the history and the types of ingredients to
use to get the best flavor out of the tea, as well as,
how to make it ahead of time, how long to store it,
and that you should NOT make the tapioca bubbles
early as they harden quickly.)

Ingredients
- 8 bags of black tea
- 4 cups just boiled water
- 3/4 cup quick-cooking tapioca pearls
- whole milk to serve (or your choice of milk)
- simple syrup to serve (or your choice of sweetener)
- For the Simple Syrup
- 1 cup water
- 1 cup sugar

Directions
1. Prepare the tea: Steep the tea bags with 4 cups of just boiled water. Let the tea sit until it reaches room temperature. There's no need to remove the tea bags from the water as the tea is steeping. You can stick the tea in the fridge to speed up the cooling process.
2. Prepare the simple syrup (if using): Add the water to a saucepan and heat the water until it starts to simmer. Add the sugar and stir until the sugar dissolves. Remove the saucepan from heat and let the simple syrup cool before

transferring to a jar.

3. Cook the tapioca pearls: Bring about 4 cups of water to boil and add the tapioca pearls. Stir the pearls and let them cook for about 5 minutes. The pearls should have floated to the top by now. Drain and rinse the pearls under cold water. Transfer them to a bowl.

4. Assemble the drinks: Divide the cooked tapioca pearls into 4 large glasses. Next, add a few ice cubes to each glass. Pour 1 cup of the tea into each glass. Add 1 1/2 tablespoons of milk and 1 1/2 tablespoons of simple syrup into each glass. Stir and taste the milk tea. Add more milk or simple syrup to your taste. If you are serving the beverage to guests, have a small pitcher of milk and jar of simple syrup ready so that they can adjust the drink to their taste. The drink is usually served with large boba straws (large enough for the tapioca pearls to go through). If you don't have the straws on hand, you can use spoons to scoop out the tapioca pearls.

Note

You will likely have a lot of simple syrup left over, which you can use for other drinks, such as lemonade

From the Author

Ever want to know how the mind of an author works? While writing Blueberry Cobbler Blackmail, I had to do more research than normal since the story was taking place in Santo Domingo. Not only did I do some research, but my editor, Rebecca Grubb of Sterling Words, helped research as well as my husband, Mike—who is now officially my research assistant since he retired.

One thing I love to write more than anything are humorous scenes. I've never done the Merengue dance, but I wanted Jolie and Ava to try it out. Mike and I had a blast watching a ton of YouTube videos of professional, real-deal Merengue dancers. I took countless notes on the outfits worn, the sound and type of music playing in the background, and the speed of movement in the dance—not to mention the hip action! I knew Jolie and Ava would not look anything like the professionals, though. So, while it was fun watching the professionals at work, it was more fun looking for non-professionals to Merengue the night away. Then, Mike and I took it a step farther by trying our hand (or I should say, our feet) at the Merengue. We may have proven to be as bad if not worse than Jolie and Ava in action. But there was lots of laughter and pulled muscles when we were done.

All the while, I'm taking notes in my journal and voice notes on my recorder to work as hard as I can to make the scene as visual and real as possible to the reader.

If you indeed find any errors in research in this

book, I am the sole one to blame. Also, I am a life-long learner, so feel free to contact me at jrath@columbus.rr.com to let me know of any mistakes you may have encountered. Hopefully, there were none.

I hope you enjoyed the book and had a few laughs along the way! I know I loved writing it and had a blast!

Exciting News!

***A percentage of all purchases of *Turkey Basted to Death* and *Blueberry Cobbler Blackmail* will be donated to the following two organizations! Thank you for helping those that live with MS and homeless youth! For more information about those navigating life with MS, please visit The MS Society's page at https://www.nationalmssociety.org/ For more information about homeless teens, please visit True Colors United page at https://truecolorsunited.org/

Cast Iron Stake Through the Heart Blurb

On again, off again, ON AGAIN—Jolie Tucker and Mick Meiser are giving their relationship another try. Things seem to be working out for them so far, and love is on the menu all over Leavensport! An unexpected pregnancy with a surprising partner, a therapist pairs off with the chief of police, and the mayor of Leavensport falls for Jolie's Aunt Fern!

Although Leavensport is serving up affairs of the heart, there are a lot of mysterious activities lurking in the air. The townspeople awake to find freshly dug empty holes throughout the fields that were recently up for sale under suspicious circumstances. Jolie and Ava *believe* they are taking a break from solving murders when they start teaching an online cooking course—until they witness one of their students take a stake through the heart!

Welcome to Leavensport, OH, where *DEATH* takes a *DELICIOUS* turn!

Read on for Sneak Peek of *Cast Iron Stake Through the Heart* Coming May 29, 2020

Chapter One

"Happy birthday to you, happy birthday to you, happy birthday, dear Jolie, happy birthday to you!" My family, friends, and many village residents sang out to me in the Community Center.

Twenty-five. The first part of my twenties was pretty rocky as I began dealing with issues from my past. Who am I kidding? I'm still working through things and will be for some time, but I at least I can see a light at the end of the tunnel now. That is something I did not have before. And light in the darkness is a good thing!

Speaking of lights, time to blow out all twenty-five candles. Not an issue for me.

One of my close friends, Betsy, runs Chocolate Capers in town and she made my absolute favorite Love at First Sight Triple Chocolate Crunch Cake. The title enough was a mouthful, but the cake . . . good Lord, the cake. Betsy made homemade chocolate icing and because she knew how much I loved chocolate; she doubled the amount of cocoa in the recipe for the icing. I could eat the icing alone. The cake was a moist, three-layer cake with the icing in between each layer. The crunch was tiny bites of toffee throughout. I'd never tasted anything like it before. The only problem is, I didn't want to share it with anyone. An only-child thing, probably. I hated to share.

"Psst, Jolie," Betsy nudged me to get my attention.

"Thanks so much for making this cake for me, Betsy! I know you don't make it often because it's a labor of love."

"This is true. But I wanted to tell you that this one is for all of us. There is one in a cake container in the back for just you," her emerald green eyes sparkled as she smiled making her freckles dance on her cheeks.

She knows me too well.

"What are you two whispering about?" Ava interrupted.

"Nothing," I said and then quickly changing the subject. "Hey, did you tell Betsy how you are such a renaissance woman, now?"

"What are you talking about?" Ava put hands on hips shifting to one side.

"What? You co-own our restaurant, your now an officially license PI, *and* we are starting a side hustle of online cooking courses for people who want to learn to cook with cast iron," I said.

"Whoa, Ava, that's a lot! Are you getting bored with your life or something?"

"Anything but, we fell into helping to solve crimes. So, after the second time in less than six months, I figured I mise well make some money off of it. I mean, we are pretty good at it. Then, when we were in Santo Domingo in February, Jolie and I saw an online cooking class for Dominican food. We discussed this as an option for us to expand and grow our business."

"Wow, you two are true entrepreneurs," Betsy said.

"Hey, if it works out well, maybe you can take a cut and do an entire class on baking," I said.

"I would love that. And Jolie, you could work with me so that we keep your and Ava's theme of baking in cast iron."

"Perfect!" Ava and I said in unison.

"I'm going to head home," I said to Ava. "We have a big day tomorrow with running the restaurant, finishing up our planning for our first class, then the big night where we start our online course!"

"Wait, this is your birthday party. You can't leave!" Ava declared.

"I've been hiding out in the kitchen for most of it. I ate and we did the cake. Everyone is having a nice time. No one will notice," I said grabbing my tote and heading back to the kitchen to duck out the back door.

As I turned, I caught Ava grinning while simultaneously rolling her eyes at me. She knew me well enough to know I always preferred being alone, and I hated large crowds. It made me nervous. My family knew this as well, but it never stopped them from expecting me to do holidays and doing things like setting up birthday parties with lots of people.

I double checked that I had turned everything off in the kitchen, since I had done a lot of the cooking for my party, and that I'd cleaned up as much as possible then headed out back to get in my car and head home to TV, cats, pajamas, and my cozy couch.

Opening the car door and shoving the heavy tote across the driver side to the passenger seat, I was startled when someone tapped my shoulder.

I turned and gasped–I couldn't believe it. "Hey Mick."

Mick Meiser and I had a bit of a history, an off-and-on relationship that as of last holiday season was off. Ava and I had left the month of February and Mick and I had stayed in contact from video calls and texting. We made an agreement we would sit down alone and talk through everything when I returned.

"Long time no see," he said glancing off to the side uncomfortably.

Yeah, that was a problem. When I got back to Leavensport in March, I saw Mick taking Lydia, my life-long frenemy, into the OBGYN. I knew she was pregnant but didn't know who the father was. Next thing I knew, Meiser was gone. Supposedly, he had some undercover work to do in an "unknown" place. He had taken his two cats Stewart and Lucky (who I had brought back from Santo Domingo.) He had not bothered to let me know he was leaving.

"I'm not a fan of the scruff," I said, noting his five o'clock shadow. I noticed he wasn't using his cane anymore.

Meiser laughed and rubbed his chin, "Yeah, me neither. I had to do it for the case. Sorry I didn't reach out. I wasn't allowed to."

"So, this is something that came up from Teddy or from Tri-City?" I asked. Meiser worked at Tri-City first, then came to Leavensport to temporarily help Chief Teddy Tobias out. He ended up staying on in Leavensport, but still did some side work now and then in Tri-City as needed.

"The city. I really can't get into it, Jolie. So, how are you feeling about everything?"

I shrugged my shoulders. "It's been a while. In some ways, it feels like a lot has happened, and in other ways, it feels like not much has changed. Do you know what I mean?"

"Yeah, I get it. Life goes on. Time changes us," he looked at me with his big brown eyes. What was so disturbing was that I didn't feel what I used to feel anymore this time.

"You said it," I said, pulling my keys out of my pocket. "Well, I have to get going."

"Okay, see you around." Meiser began walking away.

I sat in my car and got ready to close the car door when he said, "Oh, and Jolie—"

I looked at him.

"Happy birthday."

About the Author

Moving into her second decade working in education, Jodi Rath has decided to begin a life of crime in her The Cast Iron Skillet Mystery Series. Her passion for both mysteries and education led her to combine the two to create her own business, called MYS ED, where she splits her time between working as an adjunct for Ohio teachers and creating mischief in her fictional writing. She currently resides in a small, cozy village in Ohio with her husband and her nine cats.

Other Works by this Author:

Book One: *Pineapple Upside Down Murder*
Available at many Indie Bookstores Nationwide

Short Story 1.5 "Sweet Retreat", only available on Kindle Unlimited and Amazon to purchase.

Book Two: *Jalapeño Cheddar Cornbread Murder*
Available at many Indie Bookstores Nationwide

Book 2.5 A Holiday Book *Turkey Basted to Death*
Available at many Indie Bookstores Nationwide

Links So We Can Stay Connected
Be sure to sign up for a monthly newsletter to get MORE of the Leavensport gang with free flash fiction, short stories, two-minute mysteries, cast-iron recipes, tips, and more. Subscribe to our monthly newsletter for a FREE Mystery A Month at http://eepurl.com/dIfXdb

Follow me on Facebook at https://www.facebook.com/authorjodirath

@jodirath is where you can find me on Twitter

www.jodirath.com

Upcoming Releases
Coming May 29, 2020, *Cast Iron Stake Through*

the Heart

Coming September 4, 2020, *Deep Dish Pizza Disaster*

Coming December 18, 2020, *Yuletide Cast of the Iron Skillet*

CPSIA information can be obtained
at www.ICGtesting.com
Printed in the USA
FSHW011943300420
69816FS